This Morning My Father Died...So What?

by

Charles N. Smith

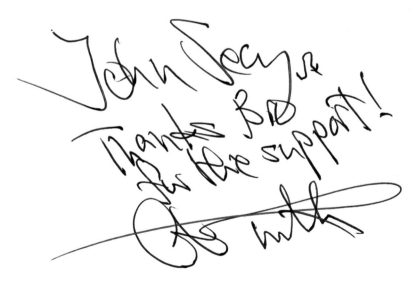

DORRANCE PUBLISHING CO., INC.
PITTSBURGH, PENNSYLVANIA 15222

For more information or to order additional books, please contact:
Dorrance Publishing Co., Inc.
701 Smithfield Street
Pittsburgh, Pennsylvania 15222
U.S.A.
1-800-788-7654
www.dorrancebookstore.com

DEDICATION

This book is dedicated to the memory of my mother who struggled to raise my sister and me, and to all the men who grew up without a father and really wanted him to be there or at least say once, "You did a good job, and I wish you all the best; please know that you are blessed, and you can make it." I applaud all the women who struggle everyday to raise their sons without a father. May God continue to bless you and your children!

Chapter 1

My father was dead. I was driving the streets of my old neighborhood in Petersburg, Virginia, reluctantly, to bury a man who meant nothing to me. I was taking my own sweet time about it, too. In fact, I was supposed to be in New York at the Thurgood Marshall Scholarship meeting, but since I had promised my sister, I would attend my father's funeral with her, here I was driving through the streets of Petersburg.

I was struck by how much this part of town, once known as Little Harlem, had changed over the years. When I was growing up in the 1950s and 60s, it was considered the hottest part of town. It was abuzz with excitement, and everyone wanted to be here. By everyone, I mean black people who were looking to have a good time. This was where the nightlife was lived.

There was a club on almost every corner, and the area was filled with shops shoeshine, barbershops, hair shops, food shops, pool halls, taxi cab stands…you name it. Some of the shoeshine shops doubled as betting parlors where people came to play the numbers.

While you were getting your shoes shined, you could catch up on all the news from the night before — who got shot or stabbed, or whose girlfriend left with someone else after the club closed.

The barber shops, like the shoeshine parlors, were where you came to get a haircut and to participate in conversations about the local high school football team's triumphs or defeats, and what the coach should have done. Or you could just listen to the happenings on the street.

There were a lot of good restaurants. You could get some of the best southern cooking and your favorite meal just about anywhere in this section of town. There was one particular restaurant that everyone considered the best, a joint called The Chatter Box. I have no idea how it got its name, but from the time I was a young child growing up in Petersburg, people talked about the Chatter Box. People came there from all over to get barbecue ribs, chitterlings, and a special mix of spaghetti and sauce called "Yak." I am not sure exactly where Yak came from, but people loved it, including all my aunts, uncles, cousins, and even my mother.

The Chatter Box stayed opened just about all night long, and it was usually packed with a lot of hungry people right after the clubs closed. Folks would be starving after dancing and drinking most of the night. People always talked about how crowded the place always stayed.

The area was built almost like a triangle with a huge parking lot in the middle. Halifax Street, one of the main streets running north and south through the city, brought you into the middle of the area. People affectionately referred to this spot as "the Avenue." The official name was "South Avenue." This was where everybody came to hang out during the week, and on weekends especially Saturday morning when people from out in the country came to town to go shopping or buy groceries. Actually, most of them did little shopping and did more hanging out on the Avenue. It was interesting and exciting when some of my friends and I had a chance to go to the Avenue. We noticed that many people there were engaged in stuff that had nothing to do with shopping.

Men hung around the pool halls or tried to talk to women who walked by. Folks hung on their cars with their bags and whiskey bottles sneaking a drink every now and then and hiding the bottles from the police in brown bags. The Avenue had such an appeal to people; it was almost hypnotic.

The Avenue was around the corner from downtown Petersburg, where the clothing shops, furniture stores, and family restaurants were. Green's Funeral Home was located on the

Avenue, on Harrison Street another street up from the triangle that enclosed the Avenue. In fact, Halifax Street was on one side of the Avenue, Harrison Street on the other. Between the two streets was a world of excitement and sorrow.

I grew up with nine aunts and a lot of cousins, and my mother would warn my aunts to stay away from the Avenue. But from what I saw, they never listened. This was where the excitement was, and they wanted to be there, too.

Another thing that made Petersburg, South Avenue so exciting was the large number of clubs and show spots where people could hang out. The clubs in Petersburg during that time were frequented by the likes of James Brown (the King of Soul), BB King, Moms Mabley, Wilson Pickett, Jerry Butler, Tyrone Davis…I heard that even Marvin Gaye had come to town. Petersburg was part of what people back then called the "Chitlin' Circuit," and it was one of the hottest spots in the South.

At the time, Petersburg was home to one of the largest cigarette manufacturers in the country, Brown and Williamson Tobacco Company. They produced some of the most well-known cigarette brands in the country at that plant, such as Kool, Marlboro, Camel, and the like. They employed a lot of people, and you didn't have to have a college degree, or even a high school diploma, for some of the jobs. People made good money by sweeping floors, taking out trash, and doing all kinds of things; however, the really good money was earned by those who worked in cigarette production and those who had the opportunity to be supervisors or floor managers. Some of the employees earned $25,000 a year or more. Some made more than some of the teachers in the school system. In the 1960s and 70s, $25,000 a year was a lot of money.

When I was growing up in the 1960s, not too many people had a lot of money unless they were employed as school teachers, preachers, factory workers, or served in the military. And Petersburg had a lot of all of these. There was another factor that contributed to the Avenue's excitement, and that was the presence of a large military base.

Petersburg had one of the largest military bases in the world Fort Lee, Virginia. It was known as the Quartermasters

Headquarters for the Army. The GIs were all over the city, and chasing the young, single, and married women who could get out of the house, especially on weekend. All of them made their way down to the Avenue, hoping to meet their "Mr. Right" or their true love. There were not a lot of women in the military, with the exception of nurses, so the soldier boys flocked to the city looking for women, and the women just loved the GIs. Strangely enough, during this time the South was very racist and segregated, but often times you would see white GIs in town with the black women.

I remember how I would listen for hours to my cousins and aunts describing what happened at the club the night before, and how similar the Avenue was to Harlem, New York. I loved hearing those stories and was fascinated by them. On Saturdays, when my mother would take my sisters and me downtown, we could not wait to walk on the Avenue. I especially liked being on the Avenue after noon on Saturday. By that time, people who had come down to the Avenue, or up from the country, were all liquored up, and they were a rare sight to see.

Now, as I drove through, it looked all run down. A lot of the buildings had been torn down, leaving vacant lots between most of them. People leaned against walls or sat on fruit crates, drinking beer or sipping from bottles in brown paper bags. Some passed the brown bags and cigarettes—or what looked like cigarettes—back and forth. Yes, there are many stories I remember about the Avenue. But today, as I approached where my sister was waiting for me, I put all that behind me and hugged her. I was glad to see her and concerned about her because I always believed that she needed my father more than I did.

Chapter 2

For most of our lives it had always been my sisters, my mother and me trying to make it. Sure, we grew up with a lot of aunts, uncles, and cousins around, but it most often came down to the four of us. So seeing Louisa today was good. Even though Deidre was so far away, it was still a blessing.

God had called our mother home about ten years ago, and for a while it was hard adjusting to her being gone. Losing a mother like mine, one who had been both a mother and father, was really difficult. Learning to live without her in my life was something I had to take one day at a time and required me to stay in constant prayer. One of the many blessings that God had provided was my wonderful wife, Mildred, and our two beautiful children, Devon and Patria. If they hadn't been in my life after my mother passed, I am not sure how I would have survived.

Mildred had wanted to come to my father's funeral, and she was even going to take the kids out of school or get someone to watch them so that she could make the trip. But I told her that it was not really necessary. It was going to be short, and I would need to be back on an airplane and back to work the next day. Besides, with all that she had going on at work, it would've been very difficult for her to take the day off without having to reschedule a lot of meetings and, worse, trying to find someone to watch the kids.

I also knew that Mildred had a lot on her plate with me living so far away from the family. She and the kids were still in Northern Virginia, but I'd taken a job in Memphis. The job was a new opportunity — and a welcome change — that had come right on time. Still, she had to take care of the kids and the house without me. I did manage to get home some months to visit at least every two weeks. But I knew it was not the same and that it was extremely difficult for her. When I took this position, we knew that it would be difficult for a while and that sacrifices would have to be made. Mildred and the kids were scheduled to join me as soon as Mildred completed a major project at work, where she served as the project leader. My situation was not much different than Mildred's when it came to rescheduling my meetings to attend the funeral, but he was my father, and people expected me to be there. The people at my job had been wonderful when they found out that my father had passed away. I had not planned to spend a lot of time away from work, or in Petersburg, dealing with this situation, but I didn't think it was appropriate to try to explain to them that my father's role in my life merited very little of the typical sympathy and bereavement.

Chapter 3

"Hey, Louisa," I said, as I approached her at the front door of the funeral home. "How are you doing, big sister?" I asked, as I hugged her tightly.

"I'm okay," she said, as she nervously ran her hands across her clothes, smoothing out the imaginary wrinkles in her dress, then buttoning up her overcoat. "Let's do this," she said, smiling gently. She turned to lead us into the funeral home.

The guestbook sat on a stand by the entrance to the chapel, with a light shining on it. I wrote my name and Louisa's. I know those books are so the family will know who came to pay respects, but I'd felt more like an unwelcome guest of the old man. As we entered, my mind started racing and I thought, "This feels so different; my mother is gone; Deidre couldn't make it. I don't know a lot of the folks who are here, and it's been a long time since I was here."

"Do you want to go up?" I asked Louisa, nodding to the casket that was still open.

"Well, we're here, might as well go pay our respects," she said,

We walked to the front of the chapel where the casket was and took a moment to look at my father. He was dressed in a black suit, white shirt, and a red tie with some small black dots in it. He looked so different and strange because I had never seen my father dressed in a suit. In fact, most of the times I had seen him, he was never really formally dressed. He usually wore a basic shirt and pair of pants, along with an old-style sport jacket. Today he looked very different, almost as if he had been some type of business man or famous preacher.

He looked very small to me, much smaller than I remembered from the last time I saw him. His face was thin, and he was clean shaven, with no whiskers showing, another first for him. He even reminded me of how his mother, my grandmother, looked the last time I saw her lying on her sick bed. She was ninety-eight and extremely small and frail. My father's name was Leon, and he was seventy-seven years of age. He had lived much longer than I, or anyone else for that matter, ever thought he would. Strangely enough, he looked very peaceful.

Louisa and I stood there for a moment holding hands, just looking down at him, and then we walked over to the left to find some seats in the front row, where the family would sit. All the seats were already filled, and the people in them didn't look familiar. I wondered if Louisa was thinking the same thoughts I was. Would it have been different—would it have made a difference in our lives—if he'd stayed with our family, or just been a part of our family after he left? Who cared at this point anyway?

Several of my aunts on my father's side were there; some I recognized and others I thought I knew but couldn't be sure. I looked around to see if I saw our half-brother, my father's son, Curtis. Louisa touched my arm and asked, "Who are you looking for?"

"I'm trying to see if Curtis is here."

"Why?" she asked.

"Why?" I said. "Well, you know, I just want to see if he is here."

"He's over there with his mother, sisters, and brothers." She pointed by nodding her head toward the front of the church.

"Oh, okay, I see him."

"Let him stay over there, I don't feel like talking to any of them right now," she said, shifting herself on the pew.

Chapter 4

Curtis was an addition to my father's family that we had found out about some years earlier. Louisa had become more comfortable with the idea of Curtis over the past few years, more so than either Diedre or me. It was rather strange finding out so late in life that we had a brother especially with all the circumstances surrounding his debut.

I remember the day that I found out about Curtis. I had come to town one Saturday, maybe five years before my mother died, to attend a neighborhood celebration honoring those families and/or individuals who had lived a majority of their childhood on the Height, those past or present residents who had reached some significant level of achievement. The chief criteria seemed to be getting out of the neighborhood and not winding up in a headline such as HEIGHT MAN ARRESTED FOR....

I'd gotten a call from one of my old classmates, one of the committee members organizing the celebration. She called one morning while I was at work and said, "Carlton, you know every year we honor some of the citizens from the Height, and this year you have been selected as one of the honorees."

"For what? I haven't done anything great."

"Well," she said. "You were nominated because of your success in education and the work you have done for the government. You graduated from engineering and law school, and you are doing quite well. We need to know if you will be able to attend the celebration."

"Do I still get the award if I can't make it?" I asked.

"Yes, of course," she said. "But it would be really nice if you could make it."

"Okay," I said. "I'll be there. If the committee thought enough of me to honor me, I will definitely be there," I said, with a huge smile on my face. I thought to myself that it would be good to visit and see some of the old gang.

On the day of the event, I was running late, as usual, and I was sure my mother and sisters were already there. When I told them about the award, they were more excited than I was. My mother had told me that my sister Deidre was going to be home on leave from the Army. After her divorce, Louisa was still living in the city with my mother. We had agreed that I would meet them at the school because I was coming from Alexandria, Virginia where I was working at the time.

When I arrived at Virginia Avenue Elementary School, where the celebration was being held, I looked around for my family. I recognized some of the people that I saw, even though I couldn't remember their names, but for the most part I didn't see a lot of people I knew.

I had left Petersburg when I was eighteen to attend college and had only returned on holidays and to spend time with my mother. Most of the time my stays in Petersburg were very short, a week at most. Still, it was good when I could get home because I got plenty of rest. There was something about just being home and in your own bed, one that had been yours for so many years. So I hadn't seen most of the community folks in a very long time.

I finally spotted my mother and sisters and immediately went over to them. "Hi Mom," I said, putting my arms around her and hugging her tightly.

"What's happening, Louisa?" I said, also reaching over to hug my big sister.

"Nothing much," she said. "Except you."

"Go ahead, girl," I said jokingly, while pulling away and reaching for my sister, Diedre.

"Hey, girl," I said. "I'm glad you're home for this. I can't believe my luck that the military gave you time off to come and be with me." Diedre laughed, and hugged me tightly. "So," I said, "do any of you know what I'm supposed to do or what's going on?"

"I saw Regina earlier, and she said that you are supposed to go over to the stage and let them know that you are here. She said that you will go on at 2:00 PM," Louisa said, pointing to a booth sitting over by the stage.

"What do you mean 'go on?'" I said, looking a little puzzled.

"I guess they will give you your award, and then you will make some remarks," Louisa said.

"Oh, that's better," I said, "because I didn't come prepared to do a speech or anything like that," I quickly interjected.

"Oh Carlton, you are not worried about that. You have always been good on your feet," Diedre said, while looking at me with such a pretty smile on her face.

"That why I love you so much, girl you always know the right things to say to make me feel better," I said, smiling back at her.

"So, who else is here that we know?" I asked, showing some enthusiasm about being here.

"I saw a few folks I remember," Diedre said.

"Oh, well, you guys know that I know just about everybody who's here," Louisa said, laughing. "So, do you guys want me to run down the list of who is here?"

"No!" Diedre and I said at the very same time.

Our mother, standing there listening to her three children, started to laugh such a happy laugh.

Chapter 5

As we were walking toward the stage this guy walked up from behind us and said, "Hey y'all, what's going on?"

We all turned to see who it was. Louisa smiled at the guy and said, "Nothing much. What's up with you?"

"I'm okay," he said, seeming rather perky. "I'm just enjoying the day." He grinned, staring at us all.

My mother, who had had such a pretty smile just minutes ago, was no longer smiling. Now she was just kind of standing there, not saying anything.

I looked at Louisa and Diedre, then at my mother. My mother started to say something. "Carlton," she blurted, then stopped. She never finished the sentence.

I immediately said, "Yes, Mother?" She didn't say anything. I looked at my mother and said, "Mother, you were going to say something."

"Oh, nothing," she said, pausing. "Oh, never mind," she continued, looking away from me toward my sister Dee. Diedre was standing there with a strange look on her face, and I noticed that it was not a happy look. It was almost as if she was trying to hide something. I didn't know what was happening. My first impression was that perhaps this was an old boyfriend of Diedre's because he was rather handsome. Perhaps they had broken up or something. I really didn't know, but after a few minutes, this guy looked at me and said, "Hey man, what's happening? I have been waiting to meet you."

Looking perplexed, I said, "You have?"

"Hey Bubba, I heard a lot about you," he said excitedly. "Man, I told Louisa to let me know when you came to town."

"Okay," I said. "So, I'm Carlton, good to meet you. And why are you calling me Bubba? No one calls me Bubba anymore." In fact, no one outside my immediate family had ever called me Bubba, not even my close friends growing up. I became a little agitated, and my patience was running thin. Who was this stranger pushing the limits of familiarity, acting as if he knew me?

"Identify yourself and state your business." That's what I felt like snapping at him, but I was back home, not in the office, at the Pentagon, or in a boardroom. I was home. "Like I said, how do you know us?"

Seeing that I was getting ready to get into a deep conversation, my sister Louisa quickly jumped in and said, "Carl, he's your brother, or rather, I mean, our brother, Curtis."

"Who?" I said in astonishment. "Brother who? What brother?" I said, raising my voice just a bit. "What in the world are you talking about?" I demanded. "You mean my brother-in-law...who got married?" I asked. "Did you get married again, Louisa, or did Diedre get married and didn't tell me?" I blurted out, praying at the same time that it wasn't true — this guy looked like a real loser.

"No, Carl. What are you talking about? This is your brother."

"Nah, what are you talking about?" I asked, while moving beyond confusion to irritation. "I don't have a brother, I mean, we don't have a brother. Do we?"

My mother gently took me by the hand as Louisa said calmly, "This is Curtis, our half-brother. He is Leon's — our father's — son."

I stood there looking at this guy with my mouth wide open. He apparently knew me, and my sisters apparently knew or had some knowledge of him. My mother had not moved, nor had she said a word, while she held my hand. I was standing there waiting for someone to tell me what was going on. But they were just looking at me, as if they were waiting for some type of acknowledgment of him on my part. My mother continued holding my hand. I guess they were waiting to see how I would react to the news.

"Mother?" I said, looking at her and hoping that she would provide some kind of explanation. My mother looked at me and said in a very soft and gentle voice, "Son, it turns out that Leon fathered another child, this young man here, some years ago, and, technically, he is your brother, or however you want to phrase it."

My sister Diedre didn't really say anything, and this guy, Curtis, was standing there smiling like a jackass. He looked like he was close to my age, maybe slightly younger.

Louisa, who was always the one to smooth things over and make sense out of stuff, gave it a shot. "Well, Carlton, dear brother, we, I mean I found out about Curtis about two years ago. Mother apparently had heard some rumor about him years ago and discovered that it was true and just kept it to herself, trying to find the right time to tell us. She told me first, and we had planned..." Just then my mother cut in.

"Carlton," my mother said. "I knew how you felt about your father, and I didn't want anything to get in your way of doing what you needed to do to be successful. I didn't want anything to keep you from hoping that your father would one day become the man you wanted him to be, or to kill your image of him."

"Well, Mother," I said. "I let the dreams of him go a long time ago, so you could have told me about this at any time."

"It wasn't just you, Carlton. I also knew how Diedre felt, and I didn't want to cause her any pain," my mother said, looking at Diedre.

"When Deidre came home on leave last week, we told her about him," Louisa said. "We'd planned to tell you when you got home this weekend, because Mother thought we should tell you in person rather then call you on the telephone. We were not sure how you would react. But we hadn't anticipated this happening," Louisa continued, as she shot a glance in Curtis's direction.

I was standing there looking at this guy who was almost my age and not sure of what to say to him. Looking at him closer, I did notice that he resembled my father more than I ever did.

Chapter 6

My mother and Louisa were right. Many years ago there were rumors that my father had other children. Several people had even said that a woman called Sister Flossie had some kids, and that he was their father. Louisa, Diedre, and I never really entertained the thought, and we dismissed the issue. When we would attend parties, a few of Sister Flossie's kids would come around and say hello. They always seemed to be pretty cool. Sometimes they would jokingly refer to us as their sisters and brother. I guess it was no joke.

But today I was standing here with my mother and two sisters, learning for the very first time that I actually had a brother, or more importantly, that my father had another son and I never knew it. At this moment I realized that the rumors were not rumors anymore. They were, indeed, the truth.

When I was growing up, I had always wanted a brother and now, on this day, I find out that I had a brother all these years and never knew. I looked at Curtis. He looked to be at least thirty or older, and I was only thirty-seven. "My God, he was growing up in the same city at the same time I was, and no one ever told me or my sisters. Man, this is some bullcrap. In fact, this is a whole lot of bullshit," I said to myself quietly, shocked at my own use of profanity, something I never did, not even under my breath. My mother had not let go of my hand. I wasn't sure why, but I suspected that she was afraid I was going to go off or something. But I decided that the best course of action at this time, in this environment, was to remain calm and take the high road, which I did. So I said, "Hey Curtis, it's good to meet you. Where've you been?"

"No! Man, it's good to meet you," he said. "I have heard so much about you from your cousins and other family members," he said, smiling with all his white teeth beaming in the sun. "I've been right here all the time," he said jokingly.

"Well," I thought to myself, "he knows my cousins and other members of the family. I guess there are others who knew about him besides those who I just found out about. I wonder how many others knew all this time."

I was standing there wondering, "How long has Curtis known about us, or did he just learn this too?" as I continued to try to take all this in. And, believe me, this was a lot to take in at one time.

While I stood there and talked to Curtis for a few minutes, I learned that he had spent more time with my father than my sisters or I ever had. I almost got upset listening to him. He was the son of Sister Flossie, my father's girlfriend or common-law wife. Curtis told me that he had about ten sisters and brothers.

So, the rumors weren't just rumors. They were actually true, and I wondered how many other rumors were not rumors, but actually the truth.

After talking with Curtis for a while, I quickly figured out that he, like my father, was not doing much with his life. "So, Curtis," I said, "What is it that you do?"

"Well, I 'm not working right now, but I'm trying to find something. You know it's hard out here."

"What do you mean?" I asked, sensing something that I knew all too well about young men growing up in Petersburg, especially if they had no education or particular skill.

"You know, man," Curtis said. "It's tough for a black man out here."

"No, Curtis," I said quickly. "It's tough for everybody out here. You have to prepare yourself for what you want to do. Did you go to school or college, you know, get an education?" I asked.

"What! Man, I just did get through the tenth grade."

"What the hell happened? Why didn't you finish school?"

"Well, you know, the life, man. School was too slow for me. I needed to be making some moves.

You know a li'l of this and a li'l of that. I tried to hang in there, but I just wanted to be out doing my own thang. Ya' know."

"What kind of moves? Oh! I know. You wanted to be hanging with the fellahs or the ladies. So do you have a plan?" I asked.

"Sure Bubba, I'll be all right."

"Hey, Curtis, do me a favor. Call me Carlton or Carl, please."

"I'm down. Look, I gotta bounce. Check ya' later. It was good to seeing ya'll though. I'm out."

Curtis took off, and I walked over to where my mother and sisters had moved. I suppose they moved to give me a chance to talk with Curtis, or something of that nature. I joined them and just looked at them while shaking my head, still in disbelief. I said, "What the devil just happened?"

As quickly as I had said that, Louisa and Diedre both said, almost together, "You just met your half-brother! Duh!" Both of them laughed, and even my mother joined in the laughter for a few minutes. I couldn't help but smile and joined in myself. I put my arms around my mother, and we headed for the stage because it was time for me to receive my award.

Chapter 7

On the way to the stage, my mother stopped me and gently asked, "Son, are you okay?"

"Mom," I said. "I not sure what I am right now, seeing that I just found out that I have a brother and have had one for over thirty years, and no one has bothered to tell me. No Mom, I don't think I am all right. The three most important people in my life didn't bother to tell me, either, since it's apparent they seem to have known for a while. No, I'm not all right, but you know me. I'll be fine, I guess. I just need some time."

"Carlton, I know you will be fine, sugah. But I still worry about you," she said. "Yes, I knew for a while, but your sisters, or at least Diedre, just found out this past week. Louisa, on the other hand, found out some years ago during her usual visits around the city and asked me about it. She and I talked about it, and I didn't want to lie to her, so I confirmed what she had been told. We decided that you and Diedre were doing so well with your lives that we did not want to bother you with the news. So, we just kept it from you."

"Mom, what do you mean? You and Louisa didn't want Diedre and me to be bothered. How could we not be? Did it not dawn on you that, regardless of when we found out, we were going to be bothered?"

"Well Carlton, Diedre does seem to be handling this okay."

"Mother, are you sure? Or is she just keeping it bottled up like she does most things concerning our father? You know how she feels about him."

"Carl, I don't know. But I hope you and Diedre will be okay; there's nothing to be done about it now. Think about me for a minute. How'd you think I felt when I found out about Curtis and realized that the whole town knew and I didn't? Your father and I only finalized our divorce about ten years ago. I couldn't afford the divorce any sooner than that. So, you need to think about that, too. Think about what I've gone through and how I've felt all these years."

"You're right, and I'm sorry. I guess this was supposed to be a good day, and now this."

"I know, but put it aside for now and go get your award. We can deal with this later, if necessary."

"No, Mother, I'm fine. I'm done, and I will not deal with this again."

After the program ended, my mother, sisters, and I celebrated and didn't discuss Curtis again.

When I left Petersburg, I was still a little bothered. I had lied to my mother, or, at least, I didn't tell her the whole truth. I was bothered and mad as hell, for a lot of different reasons. Curtis had spent his whole life, apparently, with my father while I hadn't had any of his attention, not ever. Nor had my sisters. I had always wanted a brother, and I had one living in the same city, not a mile away, and never knew it. I just wondered, "How many other people in the city knew this? What were they thinking when they saw my mother, a single mom, struggling trying to raise three children on her own? My mother constantly went without so that we could have. She never wanted us to know that we were poor, but I knew better. We must've been the talk of the town."

Thinking about this just made me sad and angry. But there was nothing to do at this point, except to put it all behind me and move on. It was clearly too late for anything else. I thought about confronting my father about Curtis, but, like my mother had said, what purpose would it serve? We were all grown, and it was a little too late for him to become a part of the family, so it wouldn't change a thing.

Chapter 8

So here we were, Louisa and me, at Leon's funeral, with people coming up and offering their condolences, telling us how sorry they were for our loss. I thanked them for their kind words, but as I was speaking to them I was thinking to myself, "What loss? We lost our father years ago, when Leon left us."

My sister was more familiar with most of these people sitting in the funeral home than I was, probably because she had been taking care of my father's medical issues for the last two years. Louisa had lived in Petersburg much longer than either Deidre or me, so she knew and saw most of them much more than Diedre or I did.

Actually, I was never really around much and when I returned to Petersburg now it was mostly to see my aunts and cousins. On occasion I came down to bring my children and wife so that the children could see their grandfather. I wanted them to realize that I did have a father. This was also at the request of my older sister, Louisa. She felt it was important for the children to know that we had a father and that we were not born without one. She felt this would also help the kids appreciate their grandmother. I didn't really think of it in that sense, but I believed she did have a point.

Because of our family situation, I never felt too comfortable coming to see my father, especially after my mother died. In fact, over the last ten years I had to distance myself from thinking about him. In some ways I felt that I was disrespecting her memory by now deciding to come and see him, especially after how he had treated her, my sisters, and me.

My involvement with him probably never would've gotten to this point if it hadn't been for my sister and the doctors tracking me down one day to tell me that Leon was in the hospital. For some reason they needed our consent to perform surgery. When the doctors called us, I was totally surprised by the entire situation, and so were my sisters. We found out that, because we were his children, no one else, not even his mother, who had handled all his medical issues over the years, could make any decisions about his health at this point. The doctors told us that we had to give our consent for him to have surgery, or they couldn't do it. This was a twist of fate, because here we were now, being asked to decide if this man, our father, Leon, would live. "What in the world?" I thought. What a strange situation this was.

As I looked around the funeral home, I saw several of my aunts looking at us, and I wasn't sure what to say. I had only seen most of these people perhaps once or twice in the last twenty years. Yet in the last few days we had been in a battle with them over some issues relating to the funeral. In fact, Louisa had the funeral planned one way, and my aunt Sheila decided that she wanted to do something different.

Louisa had talked with my father before he died, and he shared with her what he wanted to happen. She later talked it over with Deidre and me, and we were all in agreement; however, my aunt Sheila, as usual, wanted to do something different. She wanted an elaborate and expensive funeral. I guess this was so all his friends could come witness how he was "laid to rest" and talk about it later, perhaps while they sat on the corner, shooting the breeze. Needless to say, Sheila and Louisa had locked horns and Louisa simply said, "If this is what you want, then you will pay for it, because not in this life will my brother, sister, and I pay for this kind of funeral."

Chapter 9

So, as we sat there, I could sense the friction in the air. I recognized some of the faces from my grandmother's funeral, but that was years ago. I hadn't seen any of them since then.

I hadn't even seen my uncles, who lived right in Petersburg, probably because when I did come to town, I didn't go looking for them. I hadn't seen the relatives on my father's side in almost twenty years. Their faces, for the most part, were like a blur in my mind. In fact, I didn't even see any of them at my mother's funeral, even though I was told that my aunt Elizabeth came. She was one of my father's sisters, and I knew Louisa kept in touch with her and often went by her house to visit.

After several minutes of them telling us how sorry they were for our loss, everyone finally returned to their seats. My sister and I had some time to relax our minds. I needed this private time because I was not sure what I was feeling or how I would feel after I left this place once he was put in the ground.

I listened to the music as the organist played the familiar hymn, "Come Ye Disconsolate," and I let my thoughts wander. My father was dead, and I didn't know how I should feel.

Chapter 10

My phone rang at 6:10 AM, and I wondered who would be calling me that time of the morning. I reached over and picked it up, but then there was only a dial tone. I looked over to where my cell phones were and realized that someone was calling me on one of them. That woke me up a little, since it could have only been one of two or three people: my wife, my secretary, or the president of my company. But when I picked up, the voice on the other end of the telephone didn't belong to any of them.

"Bubba, is that you?"

One of my sisters? But, no, not Louisa's or Diedre's voice.

"Who is this?" I demanded, with more than a little irritation in my voice.

"Bubba is that you? Is this Bubba?"

"Who is this?" I demanded again.

"Mrs. Roberts, an old friend of your father."

Ah, Sister Flossie.

I'd found out her real name one day when I was in Petersburg appearing on television on a local news show. Some of her friends had seen me, and, recognizing my name, they'd called her. I'd been given an award for a case that I had worked on for the government. She sent me a note congratulating me and signed it *Mrs. Roberts*. I'd had to call Louisa to find out who the note was from.

"We've been trying to reach you all morning," she said in a slight panic.

"Who's been trying to reach me all morning, and why?"

"Your aunt Sheila and I have been trying to reach you and your sisters."

"Why?" I asked impatiently, as I sat up in the bed and turned on the light.

"Well, to tell you that your father died this morning."

"He what!" I said, before I could catch myself.

"He passed away this morning," she repeated.

"He did what?" I said again.

"Yes, your father is gone," she said, softly now.

"What do you mean he died this morning?" I asked. "Look," I said. "I just talked to Louisa about two weeks ago, and she told me that Leon was doing okay."

"Well, Bubba, he died this morning a little after five." "Three days ago," she went on, "one of the attendants at the nursing home went to give him his medicine and noticed that he was having problems breathing. She called the paramedics, and they rushed him to the hospital. The doctors performed a small procedure to open his throat so that he could swallow, and they gave him some medicine that would help reduce the swelling in his throat. After three days they released him, thinking they'd corrected the problem. It was a minor procedure, according to the doctor. They thought he was okay to go back to the nursing home. But last night, they took him back to the hospital because he was having trouble getting his food down and apparently his esophagus was almost closed. They tried to open it slightly and thought they had opened it enough for him to breathe during the night and had planned to operate in the morning after they got in touch with the surgeon. But they also had to get in touch with you guys because it was a more serious operation, and they needed your permission."

Louisa, Deidre, and I had been paying for Leon's care for years. I'd never thought it was fair. Leon hadn't paid a dime to our mother for us when we were growing up, and he hadn't paid a lick of attention, either. But, evidently, we were the only ones who'd made enough of ourselves to be able to pick up the slack.

"Apparently," Sister Flossie went on, "during the night the problem recurred, and they were trying to fix it temporarily, but his heart gave out. He had a heart attack and died this morning." She paused for moment, obviously shaken from having to revisit the incident and then said, "When can you get here?"

She caught me completely off guard. I'd never given a thought to planning for Leon's death. He was so little a part of my life that I'd never considered it.

"I don't know" I said quickly. I was unsure of what to say and what to do. I needed time to think. Trying to get myself together, and forcing myself to focus on the voice on the phone, I heard her say in a very demanding tone, "Well, you need to get here, because they can't do anything until they talk to you or your sisters,"

I sat for a minute trying to decide how to answer her...exactly what I would say. I needed to get myself together and answer her. "Well," I said again. But nothing else came out. I wasn't sure what to say. I was still in shock partly because of the news that he had died, but even more astounding was that she was the one calling me, asking me when I was coming home to deal with this. I didn't know her like that, and she didn't know me or my sisters like that... We weren't family, and I resented what she was saying and the way she was saying it. "Let me work some things out. I'll try to get there tomorrow."

"Okay, Bubba, I'll tell your aunt that you're coming tomorrow. I'll see you when you get here. Bubba, I'm very sorry for your loss." She hung up the phone.

Huh! She hadn't been sorry for my loss all those years ago when my father had taken up with her and abandoned us. She wasn't sorry enough to take personal responsibility for him. What a sorry lot they'd all turned out to be, I thought. And that was the first inkling I had that we might just have been better off without Leon all those years. But I was too astonished, too angry to process it.

Chapter 11

After she hung up the phone, I thought to myself, "What just happened?" I started walking through my apartment, from room to room; I finally realized that I was walking through the house and hadn't put on any clothes. I wasn't sure why I was walking, but I was walking. I said to myself, "You knew this day had to come. What's wrong with you? Okay, so now what? I don't know. What's going on?" All of sudden, I started to tear up. I quickly wrapped my arms around myself, moving one hand to my face, as if in an effort to keep the tears from coming out of my eyes. I didn't want to cry for him. Why was I crying? I continued to hold myself for awhile, trying to compose myself while periodically wiping the water from my face that the tears had left.

"What's wrong with you?" I asked myself. "You don't need to be feeling like this—whatever *this* is. Get yourself together," I said.

I picked up the telephone and called Mildred, who was already at work. When she picked up the telephone, I said very quietly, "My father died this morning. I just got the call."

"What happened?" she asked. "How did you find out? Who called you? Louisa?"

"No," I said. "Louisa didn't call; Mrs. Roberts did."

"Who's Mrs. Roberts?"

"You know, the woman I told you about. We called her Sister Flossie."

"Oh! You mean your half-brother's mother?"

"Yeah, that's her."

"Why did she call you?"

"Well, I guess because they couldn't find Louisa."

"Wait a minute, baby. Are you all right."

"Well, I thought I was. But I'm not particularly sure, and I don't know why."

"Well, he was your father."

"Yeah, right," I said sarcastically. "My mother's sperm donor."

"Well, Carlton, be that as it may, he was still your father. You're bound to have some unexpected emotions."

"Yeah, I know. But I have always had a feeling this would happen—not him dying, but us being called to deal with this. My sisters and I talked about this very thing."

"Well," Mildred said, "let's worry about that later. Have you called your sisters?"

"No, because I don't know how to get in touch with Louisa. She just moved to Texas, and her cell phone is disconnected. I can't find the other number she gave me. Deidre is in Germany and, believe it or not, I can't find her number either. In the last few minutes, I have not been able to find anything I need."

"I know, baby, but you'll be allright," she said.

"You know," I said, "Louisa and Deidre, both of them have moved since we last talked."

"Wait," Mildred said. "I think I have Louisa's new number. Let me look and see."

"Are you sure you're okay?" she asked again with an air of concern.

Tears started rolling down my cheeks again. My eyes were cloudy now from crying. "I don't know why I'm crying; the man never did a thing for me or my sisters. Give me a minute, please," I said.

"Hey baby, look," Mildred replied. "Take as much time as you need. I'm not going anywhere, I understand, and I'm here for you. We'll get through this together."

"Okay," I said. "I'm all right."

"Baby, let me look in my telephone book to see if I have Louisa's number. Do you need me to stay on the line with you? Or can I call you right back?"

"No, baby, just call me right back, its okay. Hey, how are the kids?"

"They're great. They're at school."

"You know, I don't know how to tell them because they were just getting used to the idea that he was still alive."

"Well, Carlton, we can talk about telling them tonight, but for now, don't worry about that. We'll tell them together, when you call later tonight. But do what you need to do right now. I'll try to find Louisa's number. If not, perhaps I still have Eric's number, and let's hope he has his mother's new number."

"Mildred," I said. "I have Eric's work number and home number, but his cell phone is also disconnected, probably because he just moved, too."

"Okay, why don't you try him, and I will try to find the number Louisa gave me last week when I talked with her."

After I hung up the phone I walked over to pick up my other cell phone. I scrolled down through my list of contacts and found two numbers for my nephew Eric, Louisa's only son. He was about thirty and had recently moved to Charleston, South Carolina where he had a new position. Louisa had lived in Newport News, Virginia, until last week when she relocated to Houston, Texas, but she had kept her house in Newport News.

I found his number and dialed. Some woman answered the telephone in such a nice voice. "Hello, Macy's department store. May I help you?"

"Hi. May I speak to Eric Green?" I said.

"I'm sorry, Mr. Green is not in at the moment. Would you like to leave a message?"

"Yes, could you have him give his uncle a call? Please tell him it is an emergency." I gave her my number, and she said she'd give him the message as soon as he came in. I thanked her and hung up.

Chapter 12

I decided to try to reach Eric at home; perhaps he hadn't left for work yet. If I wasn't successful, I would have to wait to hear from Mildred before I did anything else. As I thought to myself, "I don't really know what to do. Louisa and I knew that my father didn't have any insurance, and we had talked about this some years ago. We had thought about getting some insurance for him, but later found out that, because of his health issues, we were very limited in the kind of insurance we could get. In reality it was much too expensive for us, regardless.

I do remember that only a few months ago Louisa had called me and was talking about how we needed to try again to find some insurance. She told me that she had found some kind of burial insurance that was not that expensive; however, as things happen, we both got busy with other things and never got it done.

As I sat there waiting for my wife to call me back, I started thinking about my bank accounts, how much money I had, and where I could get more, if necessary. However, all the while I was hoping that it wouldn't come down to my sisters and me paying for his funeral.

"Why should we?" I thought to myself. "Why should we have to pay for his funeral? He never paid for anything for either of us. Not one brown penny." I thought about the day I had to tell my daughter how less than ideal my relationship with her grandfather had been.

It was about three years ago, and my daughter Patria was about ten and my son Devon was twelve. We had just finished decorating the Christmas tree and were sitting by the tree, talking. Devon left the room to watch television, but Patria stayed behind. Out of the blue, she said, "So, Dad, what kinds of gifts did your dad give you for Christmas?"

"What?" I snapped. The question had caught me off guard.

Patria looked at me and repeated her question as if she hadn't noticed my tone. "What did your dad used to give you for Christmas when you were growing up?"

I paused for a minute, trying to think of what to say. I was not sure how to answer the question.

I thought for long while, I guess, not realizing that it had been a few minutes since she'd asked the question. Patria touched my arm and said, "Dad, I asked you a question."

"Oh, I'm sorry darling," I said. "What did you ask me?" I was stalling. What would I say? How would I answer her question? The truth was, my father never gave me anything at any time, not at Christmas, not on my birthday, not at graduation, nor at any other time. How would I tell my daughter this?

"Dad," she said. "I asked you what kind of gifts your dad gave you for Christmas."

I thought the truth was best, but I tried to laugh it off. "My father never gave me anything for Christmas."

"Oh come on, Dad, stop playing. What do you mean your daddy never gave you anything for Christmas?" she said, rolling her eyes.

"No baby, he never did, not once."

"Never?" she said.

"Not ever."

She stood there looking at me for a minute with this look on her face....Shock? Disappointment? Incredulity? After a few minutes of examining my face for some sort of reaction and staring me straight in the eyes, she finally said, "You're still joking with me, Dad, right?"

"No baby, I'm not joking."

"He never gave you, Aunt Louisa, or Aunt Diedre anything? Not ever?" She now sounded disturbed and concerned.

"No baby, not ever."

Then my daughter said something I totally didn't expect her to say, even though I didn't know what to expect. "Dad, I'm very sorry," she said, as she placed her arms around my neck and pulled me close to her.

"That's okay," I said. "Your grandmother gave me plenty."

She never brought up the conversation again. I'm not sure whether she told her brother, but he never mentioned it, either. Even when I would take them to see him at the nursing home, they never brought it up. I, of course, always worried because I never wanted to influence their perceptions of him. I wanted them to at least see their grandfather. He was old and could barely walk. Problems with his legs caused him to use a wheelchair to get around most of the time. He smoked constantly, and Patria would always say to him, "You know you shouldn't smoke; it is bad for you, and it has been known to cause cancer."

His usual response was, "Yeah, baby, you're right, but it's too late for me now."

Patria, however, would not take no for an answer. She would say, "Granddaddy, you still should stop." It was amazing to watch his face when they called him Granddaddy. It was almost as if a bright light was shining on his face.

The day I had to tell Patria about what my father had given me for Christmas was a very sad day for me. To look in the face of one of your children and tell them that their grandfather had never given their father or aunts anything was difficult. But it was the truth. I had never lied to them, and I was not going to start now by trying to spare him some embarrassment that he probably couldn't care less about.

Chapter 13

While waiting for either my wife or nephew to call me back so I could get the number to call Louisa, I desperately felt like I needed to talk to my big sister. She would know how to handle this. She would know how to get in touch with Deidre, too. So I waited, not sure of what to do.

My wife called me back later that morning, just to check up on me, and said that she was still trying to find my sister's number. My secretary had called me several times to make sure I was okay. The word had spread like wildfire around my office, and to some of the other offices, about my father's death. People had already started calling with their condolences. They were all very nice and sympathetic.

Later in the morning I got a call from Richard, my boss. "Carlton," he said, "I'm sorry to hear about your father. If there is anything I can do, let me know. I know how these things are because I lost my father some years ago, so take all the time you need. If there is anything that you need me to do, please don't hesitate to call me."

"Thanks Richard," I said. "I appreciate your concern and understanding. I'm okay, just waiting to talk to my sisters so we can figure out how to handle things."

"Okay, man, if there is anything I can do, as I said before, please let me know. I'll talk to you later."

I couldn't tell my boss that I didn't really want to be dealing with this. I didn't know how I was feeling. I was almost certain, though, that it was nothing like what Richard had felt when his father died.

I guess everybody wanted to help. When you lose a father, mother, or someone else you're close to, people expect you to have some feelings of mourning or loss. I, on the other hand, wasn't sure what I was feeling. One thing for sure, I was thinking about how we were going to bury him, since my sister had never purchased that insurance policy. I knew that it would eventually fall on us. I wasn't happy about this because I would now have to make arrangements for a man that never did one thing for me. He never showed up for my football games, basketball games, wrestling matches, or any other thing that I ever did. "God," I said out loud, "I sure wish my sisters would hurry up and call. I need to talk to them."

Chapter 14

It must have been a little after noon when Mildred finally called me back with Louisa's number.

Earlier, before Mildred called, I had gotten another call from Mrs. Roberts, in Petersburg. "Bubba," she said, "Your aunt Sheila needs to talk with you. You need to give her a call because she wants to know what you and your sisters are going to do about your father's burial."

I thought to myself, "Why doesn't Sheila just call me herself instead of having this woman call, especially since she's not family." But I held my tongue.

"I'll call her as soon as I talk with Louisa. We are trying to get in touch with Deidre. She's in Germany. As soon as I talk with Louisa and Deidre, we'll call Sheila. Tell Sheila, okay? Thanks. Bye." I hung up the phone.

I dialed Louisa's number, and it rang several times before someone finally picked it up. "Hello," I said. "May I speak to Louisa Green?"

"Who's this?" the voice on the other end of the telephone asked.

"John," I said. "Is this you?"

"Yeah. Who's this?"

"John, this is Carlton. You know, Louisa 's brother. Where's Louisa?"

"Hey man, how're you doing? I didn't catch your voice."

"Hi, John. I'm okay, but I need to speak to Louisa. It's really important. I mean, really important."

"Okay, hold on. Let me get her." John was Louisa's first love and Eric's father. After about thirty years and several marriages between them, they were trying to recapture some old love. Finally I heard my sister on the other end of the telephone.

"What's wrong?" she said immediately.

"Well, it's just that ...well, Leon died this morning."

"Oh my God, Carlton, what happened?"

"Well, according to Mrs. Roberts..."

"According to who?"

"You know, Mrs. Roberts, Sister Flossie, Leon's ...woman, Curtis's mother. She called me this morning on my cell phone while I was still sleeping. She told me that Leon had died, and we needed to come home so we can decide what we're going to do."

There was a long silence. "Hey, sis, are you okay?" I could hear her breathing, but she was not saying anything. "Are you crying?"

"I'm okay, Carlton, I just got a little emotional there for a minute. But I'm okay."

"Hey sis, I did the same thing. I'm not sure why, but I guess because he was our father, even if he didn't do a damn thing. Look, Sister Flossie said that Sheila wanted you to call her, so she would know what we wanted to do about the funeral."

"I don't want to do a damn thang," Louisa cried.

"Well, you need to call her anyway. We also need to try to reach Deidre," I said.

"I don't know why it's our problem because, if you remember, we decided a long time ago what we were going to do."

"I do remember. But you probably need to remind her so she'll stop having people call me. I don't know what that's about."

"Okay. But look, Carlton, you go ahead and call Diedre. I'll call Sheila."

Chapter 15

Later that afternoon, I was able to set up a three-way conference call with Louisa, Deidre, and me.

When Deidre picked up the telephone, she was all excited and said, "Hey, you two, I've been missing you guys. Are you guys okay? What's going on back home? Anything good?"

"Hey, Diedre, what's up girl?" I said. "I've missed you, too."

"Hey, baby sister," Louisa said. "Ditto. What's going on over there in Germany?"

"You know, it's cold and rainy, and the Army is trying to work my butt off," she chuckled. "Why are you two calling me out of the blue?" Diedre asked. "It is seldom that I get to hear from both of you at the same time. And I know you two could care less about the weather in Germany," she said.

"Oh well, we miss our baby sister," I said, trying to add some laughter.

"Give me a break, and you are the baby, baby boy," she said, laughing even louder. "So," she said. "What's the real reason you two are calling me?"

"Hey, something has happened at home, and we wanted to call you together so we could all talk about it," I said, sounding more serious now.

"What's up?" she said, jumping right in.

"Diedre, Leon died this morning," Louisa quickly added.

"Who?" Diedre said, acting as if she hadn't heard what Louisa had said.

"Come on, Diedre. Leon, your father. Remember? He died this morning," I said, becoming a little impatient.

"Excuse me. I didn't know we still had a father, or ever had a father," Diedre replied, sounding very cold.

"Hey, baby girl," Louisa said. "I understand."

"You know I understand, too," I interjected. "But it is what it is. He's dead, and we have to do something about his funeral."

"Why us?" Diedre asked. "He never did anything for us. Let the people he spent all his time with bury him. I'm sorry—this shouldn't even be our problem."

"Come on, Sis," I said. "I know, but…"

"But what, Carl?" Diedre screamed. "Where was he when we needed him? Okay, forget Louisa and me. Where was he when you needed him? Louisa and I had Mom, but you had nothing but women, and he never came, not once. I don't care what happens to him. He can rot in Hell, for all I care!"

"I know Diedre, but they expect us to handle this," I said as gently as possible, trying to find a way to convince her.

"Who expects us to handle this?" Diedre raged. "Our relatives? Oh, the same ones who never gave a good goddamn about whether we lived or died? Or the same folks who knew our father was living with Sister Flossie, or somebody up on the Height who never came to see how we were doing?

"Lou," Diedre said. "I know you are the oldest, and they always expect you to do the right thing. You have been basically taking care of Leon for the last few years, but it shouldn't be our problem, even though the doctors and social workers made it our problem. Besides, what would Mom think? She would probably turn over in her grave thinking about her children taking care of the man who left us with nothing."

We could hear Diedre crying now, and we couldn't comfort her because she was too far away. Louisa and I knew she was angry and had been angry for a long time. Now she was in pain, and we couldn't comfort her. All we could do was pray and hope God would give her peace.

"Hey, Diedre, I love you, girl, and I miss you," I said. "It's okay to cry because I shed some tears this morning myself. I am not exactly sure why, but I guess he was one of the two people who brought us into this world, and he is the last to go. Now, both of the people who brought us into the world are gone, and it's just us. So, go ahead and cry because I know how you feel. You know how Mom would have felt about this. She would tell us to do the right thing. Remember, she always reminded us of the scripture from Ephesians 6:1-2, where the Bible says 'Honor your father and mother.'"

Louisa said nothing, and Diedre remained very quiet, but I could hear her sniffling. She was trying to get herself together. Louisa finally broke the silence and said, "Carlton, I also re-member something in that scripture where it said that 'the father shouldn't provoke his children.'"

"Look out," I said. "Big sister has been reading her Bible. I doubt that Leon ever read the Bible."

I decided to change the subject. "Diedre, when can you get home?"

"I'm not sure, I guess I could catch a hop and get there in a day or two," she said.

"Okay," Louisa said.

"So, we are all going to meet when?" I asked, trying again to move us toward some kind of action.

"I don't know," Louisa said. "I need to talk to Sheila and decide when we are going to have the funeral, that is, if we want a service."

"What do you mean?" I said.

"Carlton, if you remember, when we talked about this some months ago, we discussed that since he didn't have any insurance, we found out that it was cheaper to cremate him? Besides, Leon said he didn't want anyone to go into debt to bury him because he knew he didn't have any insurance. So, I talked with the fu-neral home and they told me that for cremation it would cost about $950 without a service. With a service, it would cost $1,150." Louisa explained.

"So, what are we going to do?" I asked.

"Kicking it back to us to make a decision, huh?" came Louisa's reply.

"Frankly, I don't care," I said. "Let's just do whatever it is we're going to do."

"Let me call Sheila." she said. "I'll get back to both of you."

Chapter 16

"No!" Diedre said loudly.

"What do you mean, 'no,' Diedre?" I jumped into the conversation quickly.

"I mean, you two don't have to get back to me about this," she said.

"Why not?" I asked. "You just said you could get home, and I know the Army will give you time off to attend your father's funeral. So what's up?" I asked, trying to be as gentle this time as possible.

"Because, my dear brother, I just changed my mind. I don't care," Diedre said. "I simply don't care, and I know Mom would probably want me to do something totally different, but I simply don't care. He is dead, and I am sorry, but I will not go to his funeral and act as if he was all great and wonderful. I won't have aunts and uncles who never came to see about us or gave us one thing to help Mom take care of us, telling me how sorry they are for my loss.

"I lost my father a long time ago and never found him, so, no. I love you two and will see you guys on my leave, but I'm not coming home for his funeral, or whatever, and that's that. I love you both, but I've gotta go. I don't want to talk about this—or him—any more."

Louisa and I could hear Diedre crying again. "Diedre, I love you. I love you so much," I said. "I will pray that God gives you strength to get through this."

"I love you, too, Carlton."

"Hey, baby sister, look. I do understand, and I love you. I'm just sorry we are not there to comfort you," Louisa said, as she started to cry. And I knew that her tears were not for Leon, but for Diedre because she could not be there to comfort her as Diedre had done for her and me so many times in our hours of need.

"I'll be okay. Look, you two go and do what you have to do," Diedre said. "Carlton," Diedre said softly. "Tell Mildred, Patria, and Devon that I said hello, and tell the kids that Auntie Diedre will see them soon. Lou, tell Eric that I said hi, and that I will see them all on my leave sometime around Christmas. I love you both, take care."

Diedre hung up the phone without saying another word and left Louisa and me on the line. We were quiet. Louisa finally said, "Let me make the call, and I'll try to call you back later today."

"That's fine," I said. "Hey, Louisa, I'm worried about Diedre."

"Yeah, I am too, Carl." Louisa said. "But she is so far away, and all we can do is pray."

"I know."

"Okay Carl, I'll talk to you later today. I love you, brother."

"I love you, too. Later."

It seemed a shame. The three of us got so few chances at even the briefest reunions anymore, and we'd just wasted one on Leon. His death was bringing back old memories and past hurts that the three of us had worked so many years to forget.

Chapter 17

I decided to just sit around my apartment and wait for my sister to call me back. My wife was working. I knew she had a busy schedule, and I didn't want to disturb her. Although I needed her, I decided to wait and call her later.

I was bothered by the conversation Louisa and I had just had with Deidre. She was so far away from us. I understood how she felt. I felt it, too. I just hated for her to be feeling it alone.

Growing up, it always seemed that my sisters needed my father much more than I did, or at least, wanted to see him much more than I. Even though they tried to act as if they didn't care about him not being a part of our lives, I knew differently. It was strange that I, being the only boy, tended to move away from needing him, or at least that was what I told myself.

My behavior didn't come overnight. I lived through some strange moments in my life. I guess I was no different than a lot of men growing up without fathers, especially black men. As I got older I found that there were a lot of men who really didn't know who their fathers were. Some had grown up without their father at home because their mother and father had gotten divorced, and the father either remarried or left town. There were others whose mother had gotten pregnant and really didn't have a clue as to whom the real father was. In the case of my sisters and me, my father was still living in the community. We knew him and he knew of us.

When I was younger, two of my aunts told me what really happened between my mother and father, and why they'd split. They told me that when my father left us, he sold all our furniture. According to the two of them, when my mother came home from work one day, all our furniture was gone. There was nothing in the house except our clothes. Apparently he had been gambling and lost all his money and had to get the money in a hurry in order to pay his debts.

According to my aunts, my father didn't come home for about a week and my mother stayed in the house with us, waiting for him to come back. We slept on blankets on the floor. At the end of the week, my father hadn't returned, so my mother packed up my sisters and me and moved in with her father and my aunts. I was shocked by this story because I always thought my father left us because he didn't want a family or the responsibilities that come along with having one. But the thought of him selling all the furniture and leaving his wife and kids in a house with nothing, just to pay off some gambling debts, was a bit much and really low, even for my father. He never came to get us or my mother, at least not for the right reason. He just came to fight and act crazy.

There are so many stories I remember that were sad memories of my encounters with my father and his friends. When we were much younger, my sisters and I found out about this place where my father and his friends hung out, day in and day out. Only bad weather could keep them from congregating on the stoop or corner. For a long time I never knew how my father survived sitting on that corner all those years. I never heard anyone say that he had a job, so I just figured he either spent his time gambling or was involved in some kind of hustle that somehow was enough to provide for his needs.

Later, I found out from my mother that he had once worked and hurt his back on the job. He went out on disability and never returned to the workforce. I was told that he found a doctor and convinced him to falsify some documents stating that he had injured his back and would never be able to work again. According to my mother, he received a disability check, and that was what he lived on. In addition, he lived with his mother or some other woman.

In any case, neither my mother, my sisters, nor I ever benefited from anything he did. Growing up, especially when I was very young, I remember wishing that he would show up and we would have a regular kind of family. Kids in the neighborhood who had two parents always seemed to be doing so much better than the rest of us.

Two of my best friends had fathers at home. They lived so much better than we did, and, unlike us, they were not scared all the time. Ronald Richardson and Edward Williams were my two best friends, and I liked going over to their houses. Their parents treated me like one of the family, and both parents in each family had good jobs.

Ronald's stepfather worked at the Brown and Williamson tobacco factory; his mother worked at Central State Hospital, the hospital for the insane people. Ronald's family was doing well financially and lived in a nice big house.

Edward's father had his own business, with several record shops, and he was the guy responsible for putting juke boxes in the different restaurants around town. His mother worked at Virginia Avenue Elementary School. They all had good jobs and lived well, but not us.

I always wanted my mother, sisters, and me to live well and have nice things, but we were struggling and my father never came to help. Growing up without a father was hard for me, and I spent a lot of my younger years being scared.

One of my recurring nightmares was that I was falling down a deep hole, and no one was there to catch me because my mother had gotten smothered by the coals that had fallen off the train. In those days we used coal and wood to heat our house. The stove in the kitchen used wood; the one in the living room used both coal and wood. I remember the big train cars filled with coal that would come through town. I woke up a lot of nights dreaming about coal and my mother dying.

I remember one night, when I was probably about five years old, I was lying on my mother's bed in the living room of our three-room house on Gresham Street, feeling really bad. The bed was right by the window, near the front door as you walked into the house. The way the house was built, I could look right from my mother's bed into the kitchen. It was a small, shotgun house with a door between the front room and the kitchen. You could see right through it from the front door to the back. I was lying there waiting for my mother to come home. My sisters were upstairs doing something, and I could barely see my aunts, but I remember that they were sitting at the kitchen table, playing cards.

It was hot in the room because the coal stove was glowing red. I wanted to get up and go find my sisters, but I couldn't. I knew something was extremely wrong with me, but I couldn't move or call out to anyone. It was almost like I was drowning, and I couldn't breathe.

My mother came home from work and saw me lying on her bed in the front room. I remembered her talking to me while touching my head and rubbing it. She pulled up my shirt and began rubbing my stomach. She was saying something to me, but I couldn't understand what she was saying. She grabbed me up in her arms and ran toward my aunt. I remember her saying something to one of my aunts in the kitchen while she was holding me in her arms. All of a sudden, she started screaming at my aunts. I'm not sure who else was in there with them, but I do remember my two aunts, Charlene and Janice, who lived with us, were there. They weren't much older than Louisa and Diedre.

Chapter 18

I was sick, and my mother was very upset and angry. She ordered someone to call a taxi for her, then she rushed me to the hospital.

I woke up sometime later the next day. It was strange when I woke up because I couldn't really move. They had me in a crib with railings on both sides. There were tubes in my legs and arms, a tube in my mouth and something on my chest, something sticky. I stayed in the hospital for about four weeks and when they let me go, I didn't return home. My mother took me to the house of an old lady who used to keep my sisters and me sometimes when my mother or my aunts were out on a date.

Mrs. Lucy Johnson was an old lady that my mother knew. I was never sure how old she was, but she was old and wrinkled. She was good to my sisters and me, though, and always had some good food and a nice, warm house. Her house was really small, but she was a small lady, so I didn't know if it mattered much to her. It seemed like I stayed with Mrs. Lucy for a long time. My sisters would come over often so we could play together.

One day I asked my mother when I was going back home. She said soon, but only when I was much better. Even at the tender age of six I did know one thing: that my father lived about six blocks from where I was staying, and he never came to see me. My sisters and I would talk, and they would tell me exactly how to get to my father's parents' house. Nobody came to see me except my mother, my sisters, and my aunts.

Sometimes I was really lonely, especially when Louisa and Deidre were in school. While I was at Mrs. Lucy's, I asked my mother if she had seen my father, and she would tell me no, not to worry about him.

The time I spent at Mrs. Lucy's house soon passed, and I was back with my mother, sisters, and aunts. It was good to be home, but something had changed when I got back. I found out from my sisters that my mother had banned any kind of card playing in the house. Louisa told me one day, "Mother said that you almost died. She said that the doctor told her if she had been twenty minutes later getting you to the hospital, she would have lost you."

"Died from what?" I asked.

"Mother said the doctor said that you had tonsillitis!" Louisa cried.

"What's that?" I asked excitedly.

"Something about your throat closing up," said Deidre.

"Well, I am glad I didn't die because I would miss you guys."

"I wonder if he would have come to see you if you had died," Deidre said, with an angry tone in her voice and an angry look on her face.

"Who are you talking about, Deidre?" Louisa asked.

"You know who I mean! Our no-account father who lives up the street and around the corner, that's who!"

"Just stop worrying about him; just stop it. Carlton is home, and he is okay. Besides, we have to take care of each other, okay?"

"Okay, Louisa," I said, smiling.

"Yeah, me too," Deidre agreed, bumping me with her shoulder.

Chapter 19

Sitting there in the quiet of my apartment, I thought about how different my life was now. I thought, at this moment, like I had for so many years, what my life might have been like if my father and mother had stayed together. Even though my father had never once told my sisters or me that he loved us, I loved my wife and children, and they were the most precious things to me. I had made it my business to be a better father than my father had been to my sisters and me.

I also thought about the many times that I had to run home to keep from getting beat up by bullies or by a gang of guys. I had wished so many times that my father was there. When I was growing up and got into a fight, it was never one guy who wanted to fight no, most of the time it was two guys or more. Back then, very few fights involved just you and the other person. It would always turn out to be you, the person you were fighting, and all their friends or relatives.

I was much too small back then and didn't have a brother or cousins around to keep folks from picking on me. For most of my young life, I was small. I didn't actually grow until I was about sixteen, then it all happened overnight.

When I was between the ages of twelve and fourteen, I was only about five feet five. Then, all of a sudden, between eleventh and twelfth grade, I started growing. By the time I was off to college, I'd reached six feet four inches. Being small and not really into fighting, I got picked on a lot. Sometimes when I was caught outside of my neighborhood, guys would want to jump me and beat me up. I got beat up a few times pretty badly and even got thrown in a briar patch alongside a railroad track once. On my way to my grandmother's house, two big bullies named Tyrone Johnson and Jimmy Jones caught me over by the railroad track and threw me in the briar patch. I couldn't go home and tell my father because I didn't have one, or at least one who cared about what happened to me.

Tyrone was two or three years older than I, even though he was in the same grade in school. He had failed at least twice, and his buddy Jimmy was only one grade higher, even though he was about three years older. I guess Jimmy had also failed because he should have been in the same grade with Louisa. For some reason, the two of them just didn't like me.

This all stopped after two of my friends and I started taking karate lessons from Coach Willis, a tenth-degree black belt who was teaching at Virginia State College. To pay for the class, I worked two part-time jobs. One job was as a bag boy at the local grocery store; the other was washing dishes at a local diner. My mother barely had enough money to keep the electricity on, so I knew she wouldn't be able to pay for my classes. My two friends, Reginald and Joe, worked to pay for their classes also.

Reginald worked at the lumber yard after school, and Joe worked at Little Wieners food market, bagging groceries. I managed to scrounge up enough money to pay for the classes. When the word got around that I was taking karate, people stopped messing with me.

Coach Willis didn't teach us to get into fights. On the contrary, he actually taught us how to be disciplined enough to avoid fights. But he also taught us how to defend ourselves extremely well. I didn't really know if the other kids thought that I had really learned how to defend myself, or if I just carried myself differently. Whatever it was, guys stopped picking on me. Coach Willis had this funny saying that he used all the time: "If you see you can't win a fight, why stay around and fight? There's no harm in being called a chicken with sense enough to know when the odds are against you."

Chapter 20

I will always remember one particular day when I was in elementary school, many years before I started taking karate lessons. It was the day when all these kids wanted to fight me after school; I was never really sure why, because I didn't bother anybody. I was quiet and really religious.

My mother had taught my sisters and me that just because we didn't have as much as other people, this still didn't give us a reason to walk around with our heads down. She taught us to hold our heads up proudly. Sometimes, this made other kids think that we thought we were better than they were, which was ironic, since we probably had less than all of them.

Some of these same kids had chased me home the day before, and I told my sisters that some of them wanted to beat me up. I didn't mind fighting one, but I knew these particular boys were not going to fight fair.

When school was over, I tried to hang around, doing things for Mrs. Giles, my last-period teacher, to keep from going outside. I was hoping they would just leave and go home, especially if I stayed in the school long enough.

I was in the seventh grade at A.P. Hill Elementary School. A.P. Hill was the elementary school attended by most of the kids in the neighborhood. My house was about seven or eight blocks from the school and I mean eight *long* blocks, like what the old folks called country miles. When I got outside, there was a big crowd of students still hanging around. They had heard there was going to be a fight, and they were all waiting to see it. I finally decided that I had to get home sometime, so just when I walked out the door, this guy named Jerome Wright yelled out, "Hey Carl, we're going to kick your ass!"

I didn't say anything and started to walk down the sidewalk, heading for home. "Don't worry, we're gonna wait until you get out of sight of the school, and then we're gonna beat the hell outta 'ya," Dennis Mason said, laughing loudly.

Jerome yelled really loudly, saying. "Oh no, son, you're not going to get away today."

"I know you wish your mama was here to help you, but we are going to whip your little black ass good," Dennis said, as he pointed to me and kicked the air with his foot, making a motion as if he was kicking me. Then he threw two punches in the air, a left and then a right, all the while looking at me and jabbing hard into the air with both fists.

Dennis was a tall, thick guy who could have gone to high school and played linebacker for the football team. He could have also been a light-heavyweight boxer, but he was still in the seventh grade with us. He probably could have been a lot of things if he had been smart enough. I thought he was a big jarhead, who did nothing but give the teachers problems all day, every day. I knew I couldn't whip him, even in a fair fight.

They kept talking and walking, with a posse of kids following them. They stayed on the other side of the street so I didn't dare cross over. I kind of figured they were waiting until we turned the corner so that no one from the school would see anything.

When we reached the corner, about two blocks from the school, Jerome and Dennis, along with the rest of their buddies, started to cross the street. There were some other people I recognized in the group and had no idea why they wanted to see me get beat up. Jerome was one of the main leaders, with Dennis, another troublemaker in school, the other one. The others in their group were Gwen Jefferson, Connie Hayes, Melissa Robertson, Cynthia Brown, Vincent Jones, and John Williams. These were some of the ones I knew by name who were in my English and science classes.

I was kind of quiet, especially since we had started attending the new Holiness church that my mother joined. Nevertheless, in school, I did laugh at Melissa when her chicken died, and she got really angry with me over it. But I thought it was funny. I can still picture her sitting in school, crying about her chicken dying. I remembered my mother cooking our pet chicken because we needed something to eat. So, for me, a chicken was just food.

Right at the corner, when they all started to cross the street, who showed up but my big sisters!

Now, while I was a shrimp back then, Louisa stood every bit of five nine or five ten, very tall for a girl. Although Deidre was not as tall as Louisa, she was slightly taller than I. Louisa walked over and put herself between me and the crowd. She looked over and pointed to Jerome and said with confidence, "If you want him, you got to go through me. Did you hear what I said? If you want to fight my brother, you got to go through me. Now come on. Who's going to be first?"

Deidre didn't say a thing, she just kept pacing beside me. But when I looked down at her hands, they were both closed in fists. It appeared to me that she was ready whenever Louisa gave her the 'go' sign.

I knew that no one was going to mess with Louisa because she had a reputation in the neighborhood of being a little crazy. Today she was dressed in a pair of black leather boots that my aunt Darlene had given her for her birthday. She had matched them with a pair of black jeans, a black jacket, and black leather gloves.

While standing there being protected between my sisters, I remembered this one particular evening when my mother was in the kitchen cooking dinner. We had recently moved back up on the Height, into the house where we were now living. It was a much better house, with more rooms, a nice bathroom, and all the amenities similar to houses in which my friends who had both parents lived. Louisa came in the house in a real hurry. As quickly as she came in, she ran upstairs, put on some jeans and a sweatshirt and ran back downstairs. She went into the kitchen and took out two butcher knives from the drawer, put one in the side of each of her boots and ran outside on her way up the street.

Apparently some guys were messing with her and had called her a bad name, and she was going back to take care of business. My mother, who was nearly six feet tall herself, ran outside and grabbed Louisa before she could get all the way up the street. My oldest sister had a reputation for being able to really handle herself and take care of business. She had been known to knock a boy out in a New York minute! Interestingly enough, she was quiet most of the time; but still she could fight, and she didn't take any stuff from anybody.

I am a living witness to how she could get because when she was much younger she freaked out on me. One day I was playing football with some of my friends, and she was sitting outside watching, while eating some spaghetti and meatballs. I stopped playing ball for a minute and went over to her and asked her for some of her meatballs. Of course, she said, "No."

When she turned her head, I reached in her plate and grabbed a meatball and started to run. As soon as I turned to run, she threw her fork at me and stabbed me in my right thigh. I looked down and the fork was sticking in my leg. I didn't holler because I was in shock that my sister had stabbed me with a fork. I was the brunt of the jokes in my neighborhood for a long time and I never forgot it. In fact, I still have the imprints from the fork to this day. That also spread the word around that Louisa didn't play, because she even stabbed her brother who was trying to steal her food.

So, today as we walked from my school with this crowd wanting to do me harm, I was not the only one who knew of my sister's reputation of being able to deal with issues, or kick someone's behind. Some of the students in the crowd also knew of her reputation and they were not going to try her, at least not on this day. Strange as it was, this group of students, including Jerome and Dennis, never bothered me again. I wanted to think that it was because of Louisa and Diedre, that they thought toughness and the ability to kick ass ran in the family.

Chapter 21

One night, when we were still living on Gresham Street, this guy came to deliver some wood. He was kind of dirty and kept looking at my mother. Of course, I didn't particularly like it. I must have been around nine years old and even at that very young age, I thought that if my mother was going to date some guy, he should at least be clean-looking and have some money. Why? Because she had three kids to feed, was working as a housemaid, and had another part-time job at a retail store on the weekends. Even with all her jobs, she still struggled to take care of us, because none of the people she worked for paid her a lot of money. I also thought, "Why shouldn't she date a guy that could help her?" I was tired of seeing my mother always struggling.

I loved my mother so much and knew that, even at a young age, I was still the man of the house. So, I did my own private-eye work and found out that the wood man was also a preacher, who didn't just deliver the wood, he owned a wood business. I found out that he also owned two towing trucks, and his company delivered wood all over town for people to use in their stoves. In those days, in our neighborhood, some people were still using wood to cook with and to heat their houses. I guessed he was okay, since we did see him in a local church one Sunday when my mother's choir was invited to sing.

We'd spent most of my young childhood attending First Baptist Church, one of the oldest black churches in Petersburg.

But Aunt Darlene and Uncle Troy convinced my mother to join the Pentecostal—or Holiness—church they attended.

She finally decided to make the change and get baptized again in the Pentecostal church. It was then that everything I considered fun stopped. We started going to church all the time, especially when my mother was not working. The wood man turned out to be Bishop Anderson, or "The Bishop," as everybody knew him. He had his own group of churches in Virginia—in Norfolk, Portsmouth, and Waverly.

The wood man/preacher/Bishop turned out to be pretty cool. He helped my mother move us to a nice, new house in a much better section of the city, called Blandford. For the first time in my life, I had my own room, my sisters shared a room, and my mother had her own bedroom. She didn't have to sleep in the living room or front room, where all our visitors would sit on her bed as if it was a sofa. This was a major upward step for us.

More importantly, I was excited for my mother. Her bedroom was upstairs, and she would finally be able to have some privacy for the first time in her life, at least since I was old enough to re-member. It was a happy day, and I still remember how our faces lit up when we first walked into our new home. The house be-longed to a rich man who owned one of the local banks and for whom my mother worked. He worked it out so that my mother could afford to pay the rent, even on her housemaid salary.

After the Bishop helped us move in, he started coming around more and more, taking my mother and us to church all the time. I mean all the time. My sisters and I dreaded the jaunts to churches. They were so far away from Petersburg, way back up in the country, and we had to go to school the next morning. Often, I would be so tired when I went to school the next day that I would fall asleep in class.

The Bishop was good to us, though, and he tried to help my mother with her bills so that she could buy us decent clothes to go to school.

My father never showed up at this house, and we had even-tually stopped going to see my grandparents. We were able to fi-nally get a telephone, but because of the monthly bill it never stayed on very long. Although the landlord worked hard to help keep the rent down on the house, it was still very tough for a single mother raising three children, even one working a couple of part-time jobs, to pay the monthly bills.

As I got older, maybe ten or eleven, I became curious about my mother and her men friends. Growing up in my neighborhood kids learned about sex. The fellows would talk about it all the time in school and when we were outside playing. So, I did know *something* about sex, and I had begun to notice the shapeliness of the girls at school and at church. I wasn't totally naïve.

I suspected at least one of those guys must've tried to have sex with my mother. I didn't know when she would have had the time, though, because she was always working, taking care of us, or at church.

I did know, however, that no man had ever spent the night or had been in our house when morning came. So, I decided to go to whom I considered the font source of all knowledge, my sisters.

One night, when we were sitting at the table studying and my mother was at work, I popped the question. "Do you think Mother has ever done the nasty with Mr. Williams or any of those guys, or, say, the Bishop?"

"Don't be crude, Carl, especially about Mama," Louisa quickly snapped. "What is your problem?"

Diedre, of course, started laughing. "Boy, you need to be quiet."

"What am I talking about?" I asked incredulously. "You guys know what I'm talking about. I just asked if you guys think that Mother has sex."

"Sure she has sex. She's a grown woman, isn't she?" Diedre asked, as if I were a fool.

"Have you ever seen her with anyone ...you know ...like that?" I asked.

"No," Diedre said. "But Mother is a very attractive woman. She's only dated a few men, but I'm sure she does more than just ride around and talk with them all the time."

"Well, maybe, she doesn't have time for sex or anything like that," I said, half hopeful that we'd drop the subject. But I'd opened a can of worms, and Louisa wasn't about to let go now.

She was in her big sister mode, using a tone she frequently took with us. "Mother is a healthy, attractive woman with a very nice shape. Just because you two, or I, haven't seen her do anything doesn't mean that she hasn't. She has just been smart enough to keep us from seeing or knowing."

"Why would she want to keep us from knowing?" I asked.

"Because, dummy, Mom is a very proud and responsible mother who is raising three children by herself. She's not going to let her children know about her private business. No good mother wants her kids to know that she is having sex with some guy. It's different if he is her husband, but why let your kids know what you are doing with a boyfriend, especially someone who may not be permanent. But our mother is technically still married to our father, and she is a good woman who loves the Lord. You two know what the Bible says about sex outside of marriage, so if she was doing something, we would never know—and that's the way it should be," Louisa said from her high horse.

After Louisa's dissertation, Diedre and I looked at each other. I said, "Yeah, okay, right!" Diedre smiled at me, and we went back to studying. I thought about what Louisa had said, and I began to think back. I had never seen my mother even kiss her boyfriend. Come to think of it, I never saw her kiss my father, either. Then again, that was such a long time ago, and, even if she had kissed my father, I wouldn't have remembered. I was almost sure she'd loved Mr. Williams. He was the only one toward whom I believed she showed some real emotion. Maybe my father had hurt her so badly that she had lost the ability— more likely the desire—to be emotionally involved. In any case, I never saw her with any man sexually, not even kissing. Looking back, from an adult's perspective, I hope she found some happiness and intimacy—she deserved it.

Chapter 22

I often wondered if my father could have been a father, even if he and my mother weren't together. Perhaps he could have taught me, his son, to defend myself and not have to rely on older sisters to do the job. In any case, I finally grew, up and people left me alone.

One day, while I was in high school, an opportunity presented itself for me to even the score with one particular guy who had beaten me up some years before. He had beaten me up because someone had told him that I was going around saying bad things about him. He lived in the same neighborhood where my father, uncles, and cousins lived, but according to this guy named Slick, I wasn't one of them. So because he thought that I had been talking about him, and since I didn't belong to the neighborhood, I was fair game. None of my cousins or anyone came to help or even made an issue of it later.

Slick's real name was Michael Johnson. People called him Slick because he kept his hair slicked down all the time. But really, to me, it just looked like a greasy mess. He was *the* bad kid in the neighborhood. He spent most of his time hanging out with his hoodlum buddies and breaking the law. Slick claimed he had heard that I was talking about him, which wasn't true. But he decided that he was going to get even with me.

It was summer, and I was in band class during summer school. (I played the trumpet.) When I left school that day, just before noon, walking down by the Safeway on Halifax Street, he was waiting for me. Only he wasn't by himself. He had a whole lot of people with him. I had Jimmy, a guy who lived down the street from me. But he, like me, didn't have the taste for fighting. Jimmy wanted to leave when he saw Slick and all his boys, and he told me that he was going home to get help. We only lived about twelve blocks from where we were. As I continued walking, I hoped he could find someone to help me.

I had heard that Slick and his boys would be waiting for me. A girl in my summer school class told me that she heard they wanted to beat me up. Dottie claimed that she didn't know exactly why they wanted to fight me, but she had heard Slick say that I was going around telling people I had beaten him up when we were little kids, and he wanted to settle the score. He was going to let everybody know that no little nothing like me could ever beat him.

He stopped me at the corner and walked up to me and said, "I told you I was going to kick your ass, didn't I, nigger? It's time for that ass whipping!"

"Hey, man. I don't want to fight, and I didn't say anything about you," I quickly answered back, trying to mask my fear.

"Well, that ain't what I heard," Slick screamed. "I'm going to teach you to keep my name out of your damn mouth!" he shouted, while he got into his fighting position. I tried to walk away, but one of the guys with Slick blocked my path; when I turned to go the other way, another bigger guy blocked me. I had nowhere to run. All of sudden, I felt something hit me in the back of the head like a hammer, and I fell to the ground. That's when someone started kicking me. I was crawling on the ground trying to get to someplace safe.

I heard someone say, "Man, you knocked that nigger out!"

Someone else in the crowd laughed, "Slick, you kicked the shit out of him. Look at him crawl!"

"Yeah man, he crawling like a dog," I heard another voice say. I looked through the hand covering my face while I used the other to partly hold my privates, all the while trying to get to the front doors of the Safeway. All this was taking place right in front of the store, and no one bothered to come out and help me. I was all alone on the sidewalk, getting kicked and beaten.

I said to myself, "If I can just make it to the front doors, I'll be okay." I finally crawled into the Safeway and found a corner and lay there for a minute. Some of the people in the store finally saw me and ran over to me. A nice old lady said, "Son, are you hurt? Are you all right?" I wanted to look at her and say, "What in the hell do you think? Don't you see me lying on this floor, having just crawled from outside, and you are asking me whether I'm okay?" But I didn't.

I lied and said, "Yes ma'am, I'm fine." I was hurting so bad, not so much from all the blows, but from the fact that I had just gotten beaten up and had to crawl like a dog to get away. I sat up against the wall and looked out the window. I noticed that the crowd outside had run off, I guess when I crawled inside the store. I'm sure they were afraid the store manager was going to call the police or something, but in any case I was just glad they were gone.

I found a pay phone and called my mother. Luckily, she was at home. I told her what had happened, and a few minutes later she showed up with the Bishop. He had a taxi and came with my mother to take me home. The Bishop asked, "Do you want me to ride around so we can find the kids who beat you up?" I said, "No, Sir. Just take me home."

"Where were your friends?" my mother asked.

"Jimmy was supposed to go get Tyrone and Ernest, but he never came back."

Tyrone Green was a good friend who lived across the street from me, and Ernest was Jimmy's brother. They were both older and all of them lived down the street. Tyrone was tough and didn't take any crap from anybody. Ernest was not particularly a fighter, but no one messed with him. Jimmy never came back with either of them.

My mother and the Bishop did as I asked and took me home. I never forgot that situation, and I promised myself that I would find a way to get Slick back. As fate would have it, it happened some years later when I was in the last month of my junior year and had been taking karate for about two years. I caught Slick in the restroom at school while classes were in session. I was surprised to see him at school. It was midmorning and he apparently had gotten a pass from class to go to the restroom, or he simply was cutting class and hanging around school, as usual.

I was washing my hands when he came in. He apparently didn't see me, or didn't recognize me because I had grown a lot taller and filled out some. But I saw him. I don't know what got into me that morning, but he went into the toilet stall, and I waited until I saw his trousers hit the floor. Once he had taken a seat, I opened the toilet stall door. You should have seen his face. He reached down to try and pull up his underwear and pants. When he did this, I let him have a couple of good hard hits in his face. First, I hit him with a left, then a right hook.

While he was struggling to pull up his pants, I hit him again in the stomach, as hard as I could. He doubled over with his pants still around his ankles, and I gave him a couple of more licks before I decided to let him go. As much as I wanted to, I couldn't really hurt him because I felt bad, seeing how helpless he was without all his boys around him. Besides, he couldn't get his pants up, and he was grabbing his privates to keep them from getting hit or zipped up by mistake in all the commotion.

Shortly after this I waited and prepared myself for him to get his boys and come after me. I watched every day for about a week, but no one came for me, and I didn't hear anything about it. I never told anyone until some years later, when I told my two best friends. I'm not sure why, but it had served my purpose, and there was no need to brag about it. I could only guess that perhaps Slick never told anyone, either. He would have probably been embarrassed, fearing that his boys would laugh at him. From Slick's point of view, how do you tell your boys that this nobody kid, whom you had already beaten some years earlier, had caught you, literally, with your pants down and finally gotten even?

Chapter 23

Sitting in my apartment, I thought about my life and all the many times I had wanted my father to be there. But he never was, and now he was dead and never would be. It was kind of scary that on this day these thoughts were crossing my mind, even though I was now a grown man with a family of my own.

The men my mother brought into our lives were good, decent men. But they never stayed—for whatever reason. And they couldn't take away the feeling that someone out there who *should* have loved us, didn't.

I thought back to my high school graduation day and remembered how extremely excited I was. My uncles and aunts on my mother's side of the family were there, just like they'd been there when Louisa and Deidre graduated before me.

I was so excited and happy that the Lord had blessed me with seeing this day. I was headed to college. I tried to put all the bad stuff in my life behind me and think only of the future. It had been real tough for my mother, raising three children, and much harder for me because I only had my mother, even though her male friends had always been very kind, and the Bishop had been such a great person to me.

I thought about when the Bishop taught me to drive a car with a stick shift in it. We had put a manual motor in a Chevrolet station wagon, which was originally an automatic, and added a stick shift. It was a crazy ride, and I loved driving it. He taught me all about engines and how to work on cars. We used to spend hours outside working on his cars, because, maybe, he was too cheap to take them to a real mechanic. So, working with him, I got a real education about cars. One night, when I needed a car to take my new girlfriend out on a date, the Bishop let me borrow his new Cadillac. Well, it wasn't actually a new Cadillac; it was more like a new, used car. It was gold with a black rag top and a huge set of fins.

I had met Rhonda one day when I was walking home from my friend Stephen's house. She was sitting on the steps of one of the houses along my way home. "Hello," I ventured in passing.

"Hi," she said, smiling. Oh, what a beautiful smile.

I walked back and said, "Hi, again. My name is Carl."

"Well, hi, Carl. I'm Rhonda, Rhonda Mims."

"Well, Miss Rhonda, Rhonda Mims, I am extremely happy to meet you." I laughed, hoping I sounded charming. "I've never seen you before. Do you live here?" I asked.

"No, Mr. Carl-with-no-last-name, I'm here visiting my uncle and aunt for the weekend. I live up in King and Queen County," she said, still smiling and now rising from the stoop and moving toward me.

"It's Thomas."

"What's Thomas?" she asked.

"My last name, silly," I said. "I've lived in Virginia all my life, but where in the world is King and Queen County?" I asked, as I checked her out from her feet to her head. I thought to myself, "My, she is a pretty girl." I got closer to her, as she walked closer to me. I noticed that she had beautiful brown eyes and perfect legs that went straight up to her well-shaped behind. The Lord had blessed her well in the right departments. I checked her out as carefully as possible—without being too obvious, of course. But she noticed.

"Do I measure up to your standards, Mr. Thomas?"

I sort of laughed, and said, "What do you mean?"

"You know what I mean. I saw you checking me out. Now tell me you weren't checking me out."

"Well, I was," I stammered. "But I didn't mean to be too obvious. In fact, I thought I was being kind of cool about looking at you." I realized she was teasing me. "Okay, Miss Rhonda, I did check you out." More boldly now, I said, "And I'm sure you checked me out while you got up off your stoop to talk."

"Well, Mr. Thomas, it could be simply that I am bored and wanted some conversation, and you are the only one who has walked past this house since I've been sitting out here," she said. "So what do you think about that?"

I simply said, "It is a good day for me to have been walking past this house and to meet such a lovely young lady, such as you. Can I sit and talk with you for a minute?" I asked.

"Well, I probably need to go and ask my aunt since it is her house."

"Okay," I said. "Go ahead. I'll wait."

She got up and went into the house and came back a few minutes later.

"So," I said. "What did she say?"

"It's okay, so come on in and sit," she said.

I opened the gate and went in and took a seat beside her on the stoop. We talked forever, it seemed, but it was only a couple of hours. I found out a lot of stuff, and, more important for me, I learned that, like me, she was a senior in high school and was planning to go to Virginia State College when she graduated. Lucky for me, Virginia State College was right in Petersburg. She would be close.

I thought to myself, "I like this girl and I feel comfortable with her. Best of all, she is from out of town and perhaps her people don't know anything about my father's side of the family." We hit it off and exchanged telephone numbers. She said she would try to get back to Petersburg as soon as she could.

I spent most of my free nights talking to her when I was not doing homework or working at the diner or at 84 Lumber Company. Talking to Rhonda was like a dream come true, and I was glad that I had gone to visit Stephen that day.

Rhonda came back to town the following week, and we went to the movies. Then she came back on a few more weekends just to see me. She'd told her parents, though, that she really liked visiting her aunt and uncle, and it gave her a chance to see her cousins.

One weekend when she was in town, they were giving her uncle a surprise birthday party, and Rhonda had gotten permission from her aunt for me to attend. It was an okay party, with her sister and her sister's boyfriend, her mother and father, and some other people I didn't know. But Rhonda introduced me to everybody. We hung around the party for a while, then found our way outside to the back porch.

We started messing around. We were kissing and fondling each other, and things were really kind of going wild. I had my hands all inside her blouse and under her skirt and was enjoying the feeling of her hot skin. Then I decided that I had better cool it. This was, after all, the kind of thing my mother told me good boys didn't do—and even if they did, good girls wouldn't let them. I removed my hands and pulled her skirt back down over her knees and started buttoning up her blouse. "Its okay, we'll get there," I said.

She got this look on her face. I didn't want her to get the idea I thought something was wrong with her. I said, "Girl, I am as hot as a firecracker. You got me all riled up, you know. But I don't want this to be ugly; I want it to be beautiful, just like you are."

"I get your point," she said, pointing down at the tent in my pants.

"It's just the wrong place and wrong time," I said.

I didn't want to tell her that my mother had drilled into my head that people don't have sex until they're married; that it's only for people who really love each other and are prepared to live with the potential consequences.

Consequences. I guess that's what my sisters and I had been reduced to when it came to our father, little accidents that he just couldn't deal with.

I didn't see Rhonda for a while, and I really missed her. School and work were not the same, because I spent most of my time thinking about her.

Then, one night, she called and invited me to her home. "Carlton," she said, "I talked to my parents, and they agreed that I can have you come up and visit me this weekend. Can you get here?"

"Yeah, I think I can borrow one of the Bishop's cars and drive up. I just need to know how to get there,"

Chapter 24

I couldn't wait until Friday afternoon. I had already picked out my outfits for the trip, and I was ready to go. The Bishop had agreed to let me use his car and had mapped out the route for me. My mother had also talked with Rhonda's parents to make sure it was okay for me to go up to see her.

I drove up to King and Queen County and spent the weekend with Rhonda, her sister Sandra, and her parents. It was the first time I'd ever been invited to stay at a girl's house. When I arrived, her parents were really nice to me. We ate dinner and sat around talking for a long while after. Rhonda's sister, Sandy, had a hot date, so she said goodnight and was headed out the door, her mother calling after her to be home at a reasonable hour.

Rhonda and I went out for a drive, and she showed me around the county. We stopped periodically and kissed and made out, but nothing serious. We got back to her house around eleven thirty, and her father was waiting up.

Rhonda's mother had made up her brother's room for me to sleep in, and her father showed me to my sleeping quarters. Her brother was in the Army and overseas in South Korea, so his room was available. Before Mr. Mims left me, he gave me a warning. "Remember, young man, my wife and I are right across the hall, if you get my meaning," he said with a frown—and then smiled.

I said, "I understand, sir," and laughed.

He said, "Good night. I'll see you in the morning."

A few minutes later, Rhonda opened the door to the bedroom and crept in.

"Are you crazy?" I whispered. "Your mother and father are right across the hall. I am sure your father sleeps with one eye open."

"It's okay," she whispered in my ear. "When my daddy goes to sleep, he sleeps like a baby and nothing can wake him up. Both of them are probably already asleep. I will just stay awhile and go back to my room."

"Are you sure?" I asked. "What about Sandra?"

"Oh, she won't get in until early in the morning, and then she'll ask me to lie for her," Rhonda said, pressing her lips against my neck. "Relax, Carl," she said. "Don't be such a chicken."

She was smiling and kissing me on my lips while she pressed her body down on top of me. As I touched her body, at that moment I realized that she didn't have anything on under her robe. She was naked. As I touched her all over I heard myself say, "Oh Lord, forgive me, please!" I could feel everything on her from head to toe. Her beautiful, full breasts were on my chest, and I felt her entire body as we kissed and hugged.

It was magical, electric.

It had to stop.

"Listen," I said. "This is a lot better than the back porch, but sneaking around in your parents' house, with them across the hall, that's not the right setting either. If they catch us, they'll never let us see each other again. I want to cherish it when it happens. I think we should wait."

She pouted for a moment, then kissed me goodnight.

At breakfast the next morning, Mrs. Mims laid out an outstanding meal of eggs, bacon, grits, pancakes, ham, hot biscuits, hot tea, coffee, and everything else one could want. What made it more special was that her mother, father, and sister were all seated around the table. I was suddenly overwhelmed with sadness. Sitting here with Rhonda's family was what I had always dreamed of. I had prayed that one day my family could look and act like this, but, unfortunately, it never did.

After the weekend at Rhonda's house, I was on cloud nine. We continued to see each other, and she came down to see her aunt and uncle when she could.

After we graduated from high school, even though we went to different colleges, we kept our relationship intact. Luckily for me, the colleges we attended were not that far away from each other. In fact, they were only thirty miles apart.

I made it my business to get to see her just about every weekend, especially when I was not busy with the choir or other school activities. Even if the choir had to perform, I would always find someone to drop me by the college to see her even if it was late at night.

She seemed as happy as I was to keep exploring our emotional relationship—and to keep the physical stuff contained to heavy petting.

Chapter 25

Things were kind of up and down during my first year of college. I didn't get to go to the school where a lot of my friends went. I was at a predominantly white university where there were a lot of challenges—and racism—to deal with. I was also struggling to find out who I was and where I fit in this world.

I had gotten a good education in high school, so academically I was okay. It was just dealing with a lot of other things, like women, racism, and not having a lot of money or other material things that the other kids had.

My sports career had not been very successful. I could sing and knew a little about music, but I hadn't really explored my musical talent beyond singing. So I was searching for me, while learning to be a good college student. I thought I had some pretty good talent in basketball and even football, but because my father wasn't there, my mother placed more emphasis on school and church. She was not really into sports, so my sports career died in high school.

My first few months in college were not going well, and the fact that I had a white roommate Kevin didn't help. Our residence hall was a huge office building that had been converted into a residence hall for men, and the showers were old and open. We slept about five feet from each other and everyone living on our floor shared two old bathrooms, with these old tubs with the feet that looked like an animal. Having a roommate was not the real problem because I had grown up with several people living and sleeping in the same room. It was more adjusting to a room-mate who was not family and, in particular, white. This presented several challenges, but he and I were able to work out our differences. I could adjust to everything except the fact that all Kevin did was talk about his father and all of his money.

It turned out Kevin's father was a wealthy developer from Charlottesville, Virginia, and according to Kevin, he was the greatest thing since sliced bread. He was a real father who had earned a lot of money building apartment complexes, houses, and shopping malls. Even though it seemed that Kevin's father was a busy man, he managed to spend a lot of time with Kevin when he was growing up, doing all kinds of father and son things.

Kevin went on night and day about his father, and I got sick to my stomach listening to him; however, it wasn't his problem because he had a right to be proud of his father, especially if he had been so good to him and his family.

I finally got to meet Kevin's father one weekend when he and his wife Carey came down to see Kevin and to bring him some food and other items. They took Kevin out to dinner and even invited me. They took us to a very expensive restaurant and told us to order whatever we wanted. That had never happen to me, and I had a ball. The food was absolutely wonderful, but I was more impressed with the waiters who were dressed in tuxedoes. When they took our orders they didn't write anything down; when they brought back the orders they had everything right.

It turned out that Kevin's mother and father were not bad people. In fact, they were pretty nice, and his father had a very nice personality. Kevin's last name was Schwartz and, apparently in the Charlottesville area, the Schwartz's name was quite well-known.

Kevin didn't do anything particularly great. He didn't play any sports either, but he knew what he would be doing after college. He was majoring in architecture and was going into business with his father. His future was pretty much set. I, on the other hand, had no idea what I was going to be doing and felt somewhat depressed thinking about how my own father had never even noticed that I was alive. All I could do was constantly hope that one day he would decide that I was worthy enough for him to find me, or at least see how I was doing.

My mother had to be both mother and father to my sisters and me. In fact, when she died, the doctors simply said that her body had worn itself out from working too much. Mother worked all the time to make life tolerable for my sisters and me. She really had little or no time for herself and rarely had an opportunity to rest her body.

There were so many things that my mother taught me, but there were also some things she just didn't have time to teach me. As much as she might have wanted to teach me about sports, she didn't have free time to spend doing this. All her time was spent working to put food on the table.

Everything that I learned about sports I learned from my friends and cousins, or through conversations with some of the older guys in the community and my coaches at school. But I never had anyone who took the time to physically show me how to hold a basketball or shoot. I learned that from my friends or from watching other folks. In school, the coach of whatever teams you were on also tried to educate you about life and the importance of school. I used to watch guys whose mothers and fathers would show up to watch them when they were playing sports; I used to sit and watch some of the fathers in the park playing with their sons, usually playing catch with a baseball or football. I always wished that I was one of those kids playing with their fathers.

Of course, my father was never there to tell me that I did a good job in football. When I finally made the football or basketball team, or even when I was playing Little League, he was never there. There was no father at home to do anything that mattered to a little guy or a teenage boy. My mother spent all her time working and trying to make sure that my sisters and I did not get caught up in all the bad things that were happening in our neighborhood. She kept us in Sunday school, Bible study, youth choir, and all other church activities she could find.

When I realized that sports were not going to be my forte, I joined the band and decided to sing in the school choir. I found that I was good at singing. When I was much younger, I used to sing in a gospel group with my mother, Uncle Roy, and some of my mother's friends. They realized that I had a nice tenor voice and actually let me sing lead quite a bit.

When I was in high school I started singing with the Petersburg Youth Choir, and we were pretty good. We got to be so good, in fact, that we became the star choir for the local gospel show hosted by Reverend Robertson, one of the up-and-coming premier preachers in the state. We appeared on his show every Sunday morning. Our popularity increased to such a significant level that the choir was invited to Kansas City for the Gospel Music Workshop, and we actually got to record an album.

The album was such a hit across the country that we became the talk of the city. We had engagements all over the state and country. Consequently, we were invited to appear at gospel concerts with such stars as the Reverend James Cleveland, the Caravans, Andre Crouch, and many other top gospel stars.

Often while performing on major gospel programs in Petersburg, I would look out in the audience and hope that I would see my father. But in the many times that the choir performed in my hometown, I never saw him once. Yet my mother would show up at the concerts when she was not working. She would always figure out, when she saw me constantly gazing in the audience, that I was looking to see if my father was out there. My sisters would also show up, especially Louisa. She would notice the same thing and simply say, "He ain't coming, so give it up." My father never showed up for anything. Even when people told him that I was singing, he simply never came.

I continued to sing with the Petersburg Youth Choir when I could get home, but it was not enough for me. I needed something different; I needed to find my own place in the world. I was crazy about Rhonda and was so happy that she had come into my life. My mother was doing better, and I was glad that I had made the decision to go to college and give her a break from having to take care of me. My sisters were both gone, or at least Diedre was. She was enjoying herself in the army. Louisa was still struggling with her marriage, but at least my mother, for the first time in her life, could focus on herself.

Chapter 26

In my naiveté of youth and first love, I hoped that one day Rhonda and I would make the perfect family—like hers, like Kevin's. I was going to do the right thing—take it slow, wait. But in the meantime I was going to jam every minute in with her that I could.

It was a Saturday night, and we had been singing at a church for a Saturday Night Gospel Jubilee in Waverly, Virginia. We had to pass through Petersburg to get back to my college. On the way back to school after the program, I decided to stop by and see Rhonda. I thought it would be a good surprise. Rhonda was a freshman like me, so she was living in the famous Byrd Hall for freshman women at Virginia State College. After I dropped off the other choir members, I went to her campus and rushed in ti her hall and asked the night desk resident manager to call her. I waited patiently, filled with joy at the thought of seeing her.

Rhonda didn't answer her page, so I decided to wait a while. In about fifteen minutes I asked the resident manager to call her again. This time her roommate answered the page and told the residence manager that Rhonda was out. I decided to wait for her since I was already there. I sat in the lobby waiting for her for an hour or more.

It was about 11:15 when she finally walked into the lobby of Byrd Hall. I started toward her, but as I approached her, a guy walked in behind her. She didn't see me because there were two large round pillars in the center of the lobby that were blocking her view. But I could see her.

He grabbed her hand, pulled her close. He gave her a leer and said goodnight. Then he gave her a lurid kiss and grabbed her ass like he owned it.

I stepped from behind the pillar and said, "Hi, baby, I've been waiting for you." I seemed to have caught Rhonda off guard. She turned quickly, and I could see in her eyes she was shocked to see me. "I thought I would stop by and surprise you since I was close by," I said. "We had to sing, and on the way back I decided I needed to see the love of my life, so here I am. Aren't you glad to see me?" I asked sarcastically.

She forced a smile and attempted to hide her surprise. "Hi baby, it's good to see you, but what're you doing here?" she said. "I didn't know you were going to be able to stop by,"

"I know. But it was on my way back. Where have you been?" I said, trying not to attract attention from the resident manager.

Rhonda looked a little shocked and tried to get herself together. She said, "Oh, I went out with some friends to get something to eat and caught a ride back." She hadn't realized that I saw the guy who came in immediately behind her.

"So," I asked, "who was that guy you just came in with?"

"Oh," she said dismissively, "that was Russell. He gave me a ride back."

Rhonda seemed to be getting more uncomfortable and started to walk back toward the front door. Her hair was out of place. I could tell she had tried to fix it, and I noticed something on her neck, a passion mark.

"I can't believe you. You just couldn't wait, could you?" I yelled.

"What?" she stammered.

"You know what I'm talking about! I bet you're screwing him! Look at your neck and your hair and your face. How long has this been going on?"

"How long has what been going on? I just went out with him because he has been calling me and he came by and we went out," she said, trying to blow it off.

"So, you just went out with him and came back looking like you have been screwing all night. But you just went out with him."

"Carlton, no. I mean, I'm sorry."

"Sorry for what?" I asked. "Sorry that I came over unexpectedly or sorry you got caught walking back in? Exactly what are you sorry about? I would like to know. My girl, who I love, walks in with a guy she says she just went out with because he has been calling her and walks back in looking like she has been screwing all night, but she says she is sorry. Yeah, you are sorry, and I'm out."

"No, Carlton," she called. "Baby, not like this. Please let me explain."

"Explain what, Rhonda?" I screamed.

"What is it you want to explain? Please tell me?" I said, trying to hold back the tears, as I felt my heart breaking. I walked out the door.

Rhonda ran out the door to catch me. She grabbed my arm and pulled me back and held my face in her hands. She said very passionately, "Carlton, I love you, baby. You know that. I made a mistake. Please, Carlton, don't leave; we can work this out. I know you love me. It was just one mistake. Please, baby, you don't throw what we have away because of one mistake. I just— I just couldn't wait to see what it would feel like."

"Yes Rhonda, I do love you, and you say you love me. But you were out sleeping with some guy, and I wouldn't have known if I hadn't just happened to stop by. No, baby, trust is what makes a relationship strong, and you have broken ours. I do love you, but I've got to go. One mistake now, how many more later, especially when I'm not around? You go on and have as many as you want. I'm gone."

I walked down the walkway of Byrd Hall and didn't look back, leaving the love of my life behind. I was unhappy and miserable because, once again, my life had been shattered by disappointment.

I was walking very slowly, heading toward my car, and realized that my legs were getting heavy and weak. On my way, I started to cry. Suddenly, I was seriously crying and couldn't stop.

Instead of getting in my car, I walked out to the top of the hill and looked out over the trees and the Appomattox River, crying and thinking, trying to get myself together. Then it happened. I started screaming and hollering like I was crazy.

Chapter 27

I thought I was losing my mind.

My fear of turning into my father, a man who had no self-control and couldn't handle his responsibilities, had cost me everything, or so it seemed at the time. I was screaming at the top of my voice and didn't care who heard me. I was angry. I had spent all my life in church, trying to do the right thing and treat people with respect. I'd tried to wait for sex with Rhonda because I wanted her to know something that I believed my mother had never known that she was more important than my immediate gratification.

Even more bewildering, I started to pine for that bastard. I was thinking that perhaps if he had been around he could have shown me how to handle love and disappointment like this. I was upset with God mad at the Lord I guess because I had prayed often for my father and mother to get back together or, at least, for him to be a real father to me and my sisters, but it never happened. I was beginning to feel like my prayers weren't going to be answered, or perhaps I was simply praying the wrong prayer. I was upset with God; He had let me down.

My life had been tough. We had lived through hard times and, once again, when I thought I had found something good, it had gone bad. Rhonda had been all I wanted, and now she had let me down, too. I cried to God for leaving me in a world of hurt and pain and letting me live through all the difficulties that I had lived through, only to arrive here with a broken heart.

I must have stayed on that hill fussing with God until early in the morning. I was glad that no one came out to the hill. As I was standing there, strangely, I heard a voice, so clear, that spoke to me and said, "Yes, you've had a tough go of it, but you are still standing, and in college and doing okay. You've never been in trouble or had to go to jail; you don't have any little kids running around that you can't take care of. You have a bright future that you have not realized is there."

I was looking around, waiting for someone to step forward, but no one was there. It was just me and the Lord, and he had given me his message. I stood there for a while looking up to heaven, then I put my shirt back in my pants and wiped my face. I walked away from the campus and did not look back not realizing that I had driven to campus and I was leaving my car parked somewhere on campus.

Chapter 28

To my knowledge, my mother only dated five men over the forty years after she and my father split. Believe me, I am a man grown from a little boy who loved his mother and watched her. Ask any boy or man who grew up living with his mother and most of them can clearly tell you who their mothers dated, if they ever brought them around.

The first guy I remember was named Eddie Robertson. I'm not sure whether he was that important to her or not, but I was probably too young to really remember much about him, other than the fact that he was nice to me. He only really came around to take my mother out, and the few times she went out while I was growing up, no man ever stayed at our house. I believe it was because my mother had more respect for herself and her family; however, it could have simply been that in our house there was never room for any privacy, especially since my mother's bedroom was usually the front room or living room.

My mother was a good-looking woman with a pair of the prettiest legs I had ever seen. I thought she was absolutely beautiful. Tall, pretty, with a smooth nut-brown complexion, dark brown eyes, blackish hair, and, at 165 pounds, she had a knockout figure.

Eddie Robertson, like the other four guys, always took me out on Saturdays to the barber shop or out for ice cream. When we were alone we talked about sports. He always used to ask me what it was I wanted to do in the future and tell me how important it was for a man to work hard and take care of himself and his family, when he got one. All the guys had pretty good jobs and drove very nice cars. It appeared to me that these guys changed cars just about every two or three years.

Mr. Wilson was a helicopter pilot in the Air Force and fought in the Korean War. In fact, they all had served in some branch of the armed forces. Mr. Robertson was in the army; Mr. Edwards and Mr. Ruffians were retired army who had also fought in the Korean War.

I remember clearly that they all had nice cars and that I enjoyed riding with them. They would always show me the city and special places they told me I should remember. Mr. Wilson used to always tell me to stay in school and get a good education.

It was because of Mr. Wilson that I decided at an early age I wanted to be an Air Force pilot. I was fascinated by the stories he would tell about flying. I guess none of these guys wanted to become my father, because they knew I had a father somewhere uptown. Perhaps my mother was not in the marrying mood when she was dating these guys. Whatever the reason, she dated them and, then, either she moved on, or they did.

My mother had three kids, so I'm not sure if these guys wanted to take on the responsibilities of a ready-made family. Most of these guys were not very old, but they'd put in full careers, or near it. Maybe they'd been married, had kids and simply didn't want to get back into it again, or maybe they still had a wife somewhere. I never knew and was too young to really understand these issues.

In any case, all the men my mother exposed me to were nice to her, my sisters, and me. Even though I received most of the treats, my sisters also got to go for rides and enjoy ice cream on Saturdays and Sundays. There was, of course, also the occasional drive-in movie that we got to see. It was nice to see men who treated my mother like a queen and also treated her children with kindness. All my father ever seemed to do was cause her pain.

The way my mother conducted herself with her male friends taught me a lesson that I never forgot.

Chapter 29

I once dated a woman who had a son. Nicole was beautiful. She lived in Washington, D.C. and worked in the maps division at the Pentagon. I met her one night at the home of two friends from church. They had invited me to a party they were having. As soon as I'd agreed and said I was looking forward to it, James sprang the surprise on me.

"Hey, man. Look, I need to tell you that Angela has one of her girlfriends she has invited, and she wants you to meet her," I looked at him for a minute and said. "James, it's okay. I figured something was up, but I can go with the flow, you know."

"Thanks Carlton."

"Wait a minute, now." I stopped and looked at James and said, "She's not ugly, is she?"

"Oh no, man, she is definitely not ugly."

"You sure?" I asked, feeling just a little bit concerned now.

"I promise you, man, Nicole is not ugly."

"Okay," I said, although my doubt was evident.

It was Friday night. I had gone home, taken a hot shower and put on a nice navy blue suit and a light blue silk shirt that I wore open at the neck. I looked in the mirror and thought I looked quite handsome.

I'd been hanging out by the pool at the party for less than a minute when my hostess buzzed over to tell me that Nicole wasn't there yet, but she'd give me a heads-up when she arrived.

I saw my host tending bar and drifted over.

"What's happening, James?"

"Everything baby, everything is good. I am enjoying life, man," he responded, with a smile on his face. He looked as if he had had a few and was feeling no pain. And he was supposed to be the bartender.

"Hey Carlton," James said. "Help me out for a minute and watch the bar."

"Okay," I said, and James took off toward the backyard, where the pool was. A few people came over, and I made them drinks. As I listened to Luther playing over the speaker, I let my mind drift.

"May I have a glass of wine, please?"

I was only vaguely aware of the voice.

"Excuse me. Are you serving drinks or just holding up the bar?"

I came back to myself and noticed this lovely woman standing in front of me. Before I could respond to her question, our hostess appeared.

"Oh, you two have met."

"No, we haven't," I blurted.

"No, I don't think we have been formally introduced," the striking woman purred.

"Carlton, this is Nicole Atkins. She's a good friend of ours, and we thought you two would like to meet."

"Hello Ms. Atkins," I said casually, attempting to reclaim my manners. "It's good to meet you."

"Oh, please call me Nicole, and may I call you Carlton?"

"Yes, please," I said. "I wouldn't have it any other way." She smiled again, and I noticed the cutest little dimple on her right cheek.

Nicole and I spent the evening talking about all kinds of things. We found that we had a lot in common. She told me she had a six-year-old son she was raising by herself. His father had decided he didn't want anything to do with her or the baby once he found out she was pregnant.

Nicole and I dated for what seemed to be a long time before we became intimate. In fact, I was beginning to think that there was something wrong with me because I was not pressing the issue about sex. We spent time going to the movies, taking her son to the museum and the zoo, and just having fun.

I didn't want to rush with Nicole, but I'd never gotten over feeling that I had lost Rhonda because I balked at sleeping with her. I gave in, of course, telling myself that prudishness had gotten me nowhere. And Nicole was hot. But I did have rules. As my sisters had said, surely my mother had indulged her physical desires, but she'd shielded us from it. Nicole would come over to my house Saturday mornings, and she would spend most of the day with me—a lot of time in bed—while her mother watched her son.

We did this for about five or six months. When we would go out on Friday or Saturday nights, she was able to get her neighbor's teenage daughter to watch Keith. When we got back to her apartment, we would fool around a bit after Keith went to bed, but we never really made love at her house, especially when Keith was there.

One night, however, we made an exception. We had gone out, and she thought that her mother was going to keep Keith and we could spend the night together. But something happened with her sister, and her mother had to go visit her. Nicole was able to get her neighbor's daughter to watch him, and we picked him up after we got back from the dance.

We had been having fun all night—dancing, holding each other and kissing on the dance floor, just enjoying each other. When we left the dance we were on fire for each other. Keith was asleep when we picked him up. I carried him into the house and up to his room. Nicole came in and tucked him into bed.

As soon as we got outside his room, Nicole grabbed me and pulled me close to her and gave me this luscious kiss. I pulled away and started downstairs.

"Where are you going?"

"Downstairs to wait for you," I said.

"No," she said. "Come here. I want you with me tonight."

She pulled me into her bedroom, and we started kissing and hugging. One thing led to another and, before I knew it, it was nearly four in the morning. I got up and went to the bathroom and came back near the bed and started looking for my clothes in the dark. Nicole woke up and turned on the light. "Honey, what are you doing?"

I looked down at her in the bed; even in the wee hours she was lovely. "I have to go home."

"Why?" she asked with a disappointed look on her face. "You're not going to stay with me tonight?"

"Darling, I would love to stay with you tonight, but Keith is in the other room, and he may wake up and come looking for you."

"And?" she said, as she propped herself up on her pillow."

I really didn't want to get into this now. Considering we had such a lovely night enjoying each other, and it was four in the morning, I wasn't sure this was a conversation that we should be having at this time. Nevertheless, Nicole kept looking at me, waiting for me to say something. I had no idea what was going through her mind, but like most women, a man leaving in the middle of the night could mean so many things. For instance, that he was married and hadn't told her, or he had another woman and had not told her.

While I was trying to decide how to tell her what was really happening, she kept watching me, waiting, and I noticed that the happy smile—and her security—had vanished.

After I finished putting on my clothes, I sat down on the bed beside her. "There is nothing wrong with you. I don't have a wife hidden somewhere, and I am not dating anybody else that I need to get home to," I said, keeping my voice very low. "You and I have never talked about my life and my parents, but there is some history that I have, and because of that I have made certain decisions about my life."

"Carlton, just tell me what you're talking about."

"Look, Nicole, you are the first woman I have dated who has a kid, and I have certain rules."

"Is my having Keith a problem for you?" she asked, both afraid and indignant.

"Oh, no baby, that's not a problem for me. If it were, you and I would not have been dating this long, and our relationship wouldn't have gotten this far." I quickly corrected her.

"Then, Carlton, just tell me. It's 4:15 in the morning. I've had a wonderful night with my lover, and now there seems to be a problem when I ask him to wake up with me in the morning."

"Nicole, here's the thing: I have always said that I wouldn't spend the night with a woman and wake up and have her kids walk in and see me in the bed with their mama. Children attach meaning to that type of thing—seeing their mothers in bed with a man especially boys, because they have a very special attachment to their mothers. They remember who their mother's dated. And until I know that I may be around for a while, I just would prefer that your son—Keith—doesn't see me sleeping with his mother."

I wasn't sure she was understanding me, so I pressed on. "Boys form certain assumptions about their mothers and the men they date, when they date. My own mother, a single mother, was very discreet. I can't say that I fully appreciated that until I was grown and started working with young boys. I found that a lot of them, especially those who were struggling with the juvenile authorities, had formed opinions of women based on their mother's affairs with men. I simply prefer that you and I keep what we do with each other separate from what we do with Keith. He's only six, but if he walks in and sees me in bed with you, he will know what has taken place. If I am gone and someone else shows up, what happens? If this pattern continues, there is a possibility that his opinion of you might change. I don't want to be a part of that."

I looked at Nicole. Her look of fear and indignation had given way to one of soft and grateful understanding.

When I finished, she removed the cover that was over her body and came close to whisper in my ear. "That's why I care so much for you because you are so concerned about my well-being and Keith's. I admire that."

She looked at me and smiled. "But Keith is a heavy sleeper, and he won't wake up until around seven and it is only four thirty." Then her smile turned wickedly seductive. "Take your clothes off and get back into the bed; we have at least two hours, and you can be gone long before he wakes up."

Chapter 30

I couldn't believe all the memories that were flooding back as I was making arrangements to get to the funeral. As I sat on the edge of my bed, I remembered one of the few encounters that I did have with my father.

It was a Saturday, right after school had let out for the summer. I was visiting my aunt Rhonda up on Hull Street, a short street that was actually more like an alley made into a dead-end street. It was located in the part of the Height where a large number of my relatives on both sides lived.

It had been a while since I had seen him, and my sisters had not mentioned having seen him lately either.

There was a lady, Miss Elise, who lived up the street from my aunt. Miss Elise ran one of those whiskey houses, or juke joints, as we called them. At her house, you could go and drink beer, wine, or liquor and listen to music and play cards. From time to time, as we later learned, you could even get a woman if you had the money.

She sold liquor by the shots: you could buy a pint of whiskey, a fifty-cent shot, or whatever you wanted as long as you sat and drank all day and night long. One of my father's buddies saw me playing outside in front of my aunt's house and said, "Little man, your daddy is up at Elise's house. Why don't you go and say hello?"

My father, as I learned, frequented this house. If you needed to find him, and he wasn't sitting on his usual stoop on the corner or at his girlfriend's house, he was at Miss Elise's, especially in the evening.

This particular Saturday, around four o'clock, I was over at my aunt's house playing with my cousins, Andre and Sheila. After the guy mentioned my father, I thought about going up to see him. I wanted to see him for no particular reason, just because I hadn't seen him in such a long time. When I walked in the house I saw him sitting at one of the tables with some of his friends, playing cards and drinking. I walked over near the table, but my father didn't see me. He was too busy looking at the cards in his hands. That was until one of the men sitting with him saw me and said, "Leon, your boy is here." I walked up beside him and said, "Hello."

He never looked up from the cards in his hands. "How's your ma?"

"She's fine."

"Whatchoo doin' here?"

"I'm down at my aunt's house. Lim told me you were here, so I decided to come up to see you."

"What for, I ain't got no money!"

I started to get angry. "I didn't ask for anything."

"And don't ask because I ain't got none, so don't even bother."

I said nothing, just stood there trying to figure out what to say next.

"Well, then, get outta here. You got no business in here anyway. Now git."

Then, he pushed me. It was a hard push and I fell to the floor. I stayed there for a minute, waiting for someone to say something, but none of the men he was sitting with said anything. They kept focusing on the cards in their hands.

He looked down at me and said: "Now car-r-r-y your little black ass back down the street and don't come back, you hear? Git," he yelled at me.

I ran out of that house crying and pissed off. I ran back to my aunt's house. My cousin, Andre, asked what was wrong.

"Nothing," I said.

"So, why are you crying?" he persisted.

"He pushed me!" I screamed. I was extremely agitated and angry.

"Who pushed you?"

"Leon, my father! He put his hands on me, and I ain't going to take that from him. Not from him!"

I went around to the backyard and looked around for a minute. I saw an ax that was stuck in a wooden stump. I went over and pulled it out, staring at it for a minute, thinking to myself and finally deciding that I'd had enough. I ran around the front of the house with the ax in my hand. I started up the street with the ax, and my cousin Andre asked me where I was going. I didn't say anything, and he walked over to me, looked at me and repeated the question, "What are you doing with that ax?"

I didn't say a word. He reached for the ax as if to pull it from my hands, but I was too strong for him, and he couldn't pry it out of my hands. I pulled away from him and headed up the street toward Elise's house.

He ran after me again and said, "Carl, where are you going? What's wrong with you? What happened?"

I kept going, more determined than ever to show my father that he had not earned the right to put his hands on me. I heard my cousin call to his mother, "Mom, Mom, come quick. Carl's got the ax!"

My aunt came running out the front door and up the street behind me. She caught me just before I got to the steps at Elise's. My aunt was gasping for breath. She was holding my arm with one hand as she steadied herself with the other on the banister.

"Boy, what are you doing up here with this ax? What's wrong with you? Have you lost your mind or something?"

"I'm going to kill that no-count bastard."

"Who?" she asked, looking shocked that a good little church boy like me had used profanity. "What in the world are you talking about, boy?" she demanded. "Who're you going to kill?"

"He put his hands on me!"

"Who put their hands on you?"

By this time tears were pouring down my face and Aunt Rhonda, confused by my behavior, was standing in front of me, trying to figure out what had happened.

"His father," Andre cried. "His father did something to him."

I noticed Andre was slowly moving up behind me, fists balled up, nodding as if to say he was behind me if this should go down.

"What happened? What did Leon do to you?" she asked.

Through tears, I said, "He pushed me down on the floor."

"Why?"

"I don't know," I snapped.

"Well are you okay? Are you hurt?"

"No ma'am," I said. "I'm not hurt. I'm okay, but he had no right to put his hands on me."

My aunt softened her tone and smiled at me. "I know, baby, but you can't kill him or hurt him for that. You have to let it go and just stay away from him."

I was standing beside her, crying and feeling hurt. She hugged me gently, then looked at me and said, "Let's go back to the house and get you something to eat and drink. You'll feel better, and you can forget all about your father. Give me the ax."

I let her and Andre walk me back to their house.

"I hate him for leaving my mother and leaving us in such bad shape," I thought. "I really hate him. He's not a father, he's nothing."

That was the last time I saw him for a very long time. I was not pressed to see him any time soon. In fact, I didn't care if I ever saw him again.

Chapter 31

Growing up without a father was not what I would have hoped for as a child. But, I guess when I thought about the problems that some of my friends told me their parents were having at home—their mother and father arguing and fighting most of the time—in some ways I was blessed. When I was growing up, I never thought of my home situation and my mother and father's breakup as a blessing. Since most of my friends who had their fathers at home had a lot more of everything than we did, I used to think that perhaps the arguing and fighting was better than having no father at all.

My mother, sisters, and I had it very hard for a long time until my mother started working the two jobs and things finally got better. I remember on many occasions we simply didn't having anything in the house to eat. In fact, my sisters and I would make a meal out of pan bread and use what was left of the syrup. Pan bread was fried and made out of flour and water. Believe it or not, it was pretty good, especially when you were hungry. Eating pan bread wasn't the worst thing; we also ate "mush," a concoction of leftover cornbread, mashed up in a frying pan and cooked with water.

One of the worst things we lived through was not having electricity or water for six months at a time. Unfortunately, it was often a choice my mother had to make. It was either pay the water bill and not the electric bill, or vice versa. Sometimes when our electricity was off, we would run an extension cord from our neighbor's house so that we could have lights; however, most of the time, we simply used oil lamps to light up our house. It was bad, but after a while we just got used to it. It was only really bad when my friends wanted to come over to our house and we didn't have any lights, so I had to make up something to tell them to keep from being embarrassed.

When the water was turned off, we used five-gallon jugs to carry water from our neighbor's or some other relative's house to make sure we had enough water that we could take baths until we could get the bill paid.

The bad thing about not having water was not just the fact that we had to get water from somewhere else to cook and use for drinking. Someone also had to heat water on the stove to get it hot in order to take a bath. In the morning we had to use ice cold water to wash our faces and brush our teeth. In addition, when we used the toilet, we had to pour the water down the toilet bowl really fast, so that whatever was left in it would go down and not sit on top of the water.

It was really tough for us, but no matter how rough it became, my mother kept telling us that things were going to get better, that the Lord would work it out for us.

Between her and the Lord, it did work out. Maybe not right then, but eventually.

Chapter 32

I was sure that Leon would come to my high school graduation, since a lot of his friends' children were also graduating. Everyone we knew was aware that I was graduating from high school.

The night of graduation, I expected to see him, but he didn't show up. I kept watching and watching, looking in the crowd, but I never saw him. He was true to his sorry nature, because he never showed up for Louisa's or Deidre's graduation, either.

When I finished high school and was ready to go to college, I was so happy. I never thought that I would be going to college. I only had one cousin in the family who had gone to college. Louisa went to community college for a couple of semesters, then decided to find a job, so I would be the very first in my immediate family to go to a four-year college.

I decided to go to college because my two best friends said that they were going, and I didn't want them to leave me behind. I knew that my mother didn't have the money to send me to college, or even to help, so I didn't know how I was going to work this out. All I knew was that I had to go. This would be my only chance to leave my hometown and give my mother a chance to do something for herself for a change. Besides, Ronald and Edward were going, so I wanted to go, too. I was eighteen, and I needed to be out of my mother's house so she could get a break and finally stop working so much.

I worked at the store and saved enough money to pay for the application fee. I got accepted to Hampton Institute and was excited because Terry Johnson, another school buddy of mine, Cynthia Anderson, and some other students from my graduating class were going to Hampton. It was supposed to be one of the best schools in the state. So when I got my acceptance notice, I was as happy as I could be.

My mother and sisters were also excited for me. My grades were good, and I was hoping that I would be able to get a scholarship. If I was awarded a scholarship, I figured it would be enough for me to go, even if I had to work after classes to earn additional money.

When I received my financial aid package from Hampton University, it was not enough money to cover my tuition, room and board. I did get a small scholarship, but it just wasn't enough. My mother didn't have any money to give me, and what I made at my little part-time job at the store was not going to help, either. I had gotten excited and hadn't realized that, perhaps, people as poor as me didn't get an opportunity to go to college, in spite of claims by teachers that there was plenty of financial aid available.

My family was not the same as the families of many of my other friends. Terry's daddy worked at the cigarette factory, and both of Ronald's and Edward's parents had good jobs, too, so they were pretty much set to go. What they didn't get in their financial aid packages, their parents took out in loans to cover the balances.

In my case, all I had was the scholarship and some financial aid, but it wasn't enough. My mother didn't have the financial status to get a loan. We simply couldn't afford it. Hampton had given me a scholarship and a financial aid package that averaged out to $1,950. The total cost for tuition, room, and board was $3,850. For a poor kid like me, there was no one I could ask to loan me another $1,900.

I had pretty much decided to give up and try to get a job at the local tobacco factory, until Ronald stopped me after school one day and said, "I heard these two counselors talking this morning about a recruiter who is coming from the University of Richmond to visit our school next week."

"So why are you telling me? I have already gone down that road once," I said, feeling a little angry.

"No man," he said. "The counselors were saying that because the University of Richmond is this big white school they are trying to get some black students to come to their school."

"Okay," I said.

"Man, listen," Ronald said. "They have some scholarships for black students with good grades who would be interested in attending the University of Richmond," he said, with a big smile on his face.

"Do you know anything about the University of Richmond?" I asked Ronald.

"No Carl, but I heard two of the counselors talking, and they said it was a very good school with some strong academic credentials. I also know that it's in Richmond. From what I hear, Richmond is a pretty cool city."

"Well, I don't care. If there is an opportunity to get to college and get out of this town, I am taking it!" I said, as I wrote the information down on my note pad.

"Hey man, this may be an opportunity to go together. So I will be at that session next week myself. Man, we can go together," Ronald said, very excited now.

"Okay, Ronald, it's a deal."

I decided not to tell my mother about this news because I needed to find out more before I could get all excited again. But I couldn't help thinking that this could be another chance for me.

Chapter 33

On Thursday I was excited about getting a chance to talk to this recruiter. I was one of the first students to get to the library; Ronald showed up a few minutes later. We were sitting patiently in our seats waiting to hear what the recruiter had to say.

At 3:00 PM sharp a well-dressed African-American man got up and introduced himself. "Hi. My name is Donald Thomas, and I am from the University of Richmond," he said. "I am here to tell you about why those of you planning to attend college should consider the University of Richmond."

This guy was great, and the information he shared with us about the programs was very interesting. Before he finished, he talked about what I had been waiting to hear. "Oh," he said. "Did I mention that we have several academic scholarships available for students with good grades who are interested in coming to Richmond?"

I said to myself, "One of those scholarships is going to have my name on it." I knew I had a chance to go there, and the things he shared about the school fit right in with my college goals.

I could feel the tension from days earlier lighten with antici-pation and my face lit up like a Christmas tree. If I could get in and receive a scholarship, it was going to be like Christmas for me.

He impressed me so much that I asked Mr. Walker, one of my teachers, to help me get my letter ready, along with the necessary paperwork to apply for one of the academic scholarships. Mr. Walker looked at me and said, "I can do more than assist you with the scholarship paperwork. I'll also write you a letter of recommendation."

I almost started to cry. It took all I had to hold back the tears.

"Thank you so very much, Mr. Walker. You will never know how much this mean to me."

"I do, Carlton, because I have been where you are."

"Thank you again," I said, as I left his office. I was astonished. Not just because he was offering to help me, but because he was unashamed to admit to having grown up in circumstances that I abhorred. I realized something else, too. Despite where he'd come from, Mr. Walker had made something of himself. He was now in a position to help others, and he was doing it—for me.

Chapter 34

It was a very exciting day when Louisa came in waving a letter in the air. "Carl, here is a letter from the University of Richmond for you. You want me to open it?"

"No, of course not," I said.

"Well, go ahead and open it yourself then." She handed the letter over to me.

"No, I can't; I'm too nervous."

"Why not, boy? You have been waiting for this letter forever."

"I'm going to wait til Mom gets home," I said and I put the letter on the table.

I couldn't be still. I was fidgeting around the house all evening, waiting for my mother to get home from work. I kept watching the clock. I saw it move from four o'clock to five o'clock, to five thirty and then six, and she still hadn't gotten home.

I was anxious to see what the letter said. Suppose they didn't let me in? "No!" I thought. "That's not possible. I have good grades, and I got a good SAT score. They'll let me in. But suppose all the scholarship money is gone? No! That's not possible. Mr. Thomas had said they had plenty of money." I just wanted my mother to hurry up and get home.

At nine thirty, my mother finally walked in the front door, and she looked so tired that I felt bad disturbing her. So I didn't say a thing.

Louisa came in later, around ten o'clock, and my mother was sitting at the table, trying to finish her dinner, which she had only started a few minutes earlier. I was sitting at the table, trying to finish a book by D.H. Lawrence for my English class.

Louisa sat down at the table and said, "Carl, what did the letter say?"

I tried to catch her before she got it all out, but it was too late. My mother looked up from her plate. "What letter?"

"Carl got a letter today from that University of Richmond."

"Oh son, that's great! What did it say?"

"Well, Mom," I said, a little reluctantly. "I haven't opened it yet."

"Why not, baby?"

"Well," I said, "I was waiting for you to get home, but you just looked so tired when you came in that I didn't want to disturb you."

"Oh baby, I *am* tired, but this is important to you and all of us. Where's the letter, baby? Let's get it open now."

I went to my room to get the letter from where I left it earlier, when I was just lying on my bed looking at it and thinking to myself how it would be, going off to college. I picked up the letter and went back into the kitchen, where Mother and Louisa were waiting for me. I started opening it very slowly. I was hoping that if I opened it very slowly, if it was not good news, by taking my time maybe it would automatically change. Once I had finished opening the envelope, I took out the letter and didn't unfold it, but looked at it for a few minutes and then gave it to my mother. "You read it, Mom."

My mother took the letter from my hand.

"Okay baby, I'll open it."

She slowly unfolded the letter and, for what seemed like hours, didn't say anything. Then this big smile appeared on her face, as if the heavens had opened up and poured out showers of blessings. It was a big smile. My mother, who earlier had seemed as if she could barely make it another few minutes without falling onto her bed and into a deep sleep, now was smiling from ear to ear. She said in a nice, loud voice as she threw up her hands toward heaven, "My baby is going to college!"

Chapter 35

In college, I met a lot of other students who had great fathers, at least that was what they told everybody. Then there were the others who didn't know who their fathers were or where they were. Some of the students even shared the stories about their fathers that their mothers had told them when they were growing up.

A girl in my psychology class, who was from Hurt, Virginia, told me about how her mother had told her that her father died in the Vietnam War. Later she found out that he had run off with an other woman who lived around the corner from them.

One day, when Gloria and I were talking, she said, "Carl, you know the saddest thing about my father was that people right in our neighborhood knew the truth and no one ever told me." I didn't mention my situation. I simply said, "That's a shame."

"You know," she said, "I found out what really happened one day when I was in my mother's closet, looking for something to wear to a dance. I needed something different, and she had all of these great clothes she never wore, so I thought I would borrow one of her outfits. As I was trying on some of her things, I decided that I needed some shoes to match the outfit. I pulled out several boxes from under her clothes and noticed a box stuck under some more shoeboxes, way back in the corner. Do you know what I found in that box?"

I already had formulated what I thought was a pretty good guess. People's secret lives could jump out of just about any corner and surprise you. I knew this from my own experience, but I wasn't about to reveal my own personal shocks.

"No," I said. "What?"

"I found some pictures of my father, but that's not all. He was hugging some other woman. There was a letter stuck to the back of one of the pictures. Do you want to know what the letter said?"

Sensing that she intended—no, needed—to tell me, I said, "Yeah, sure."

"To my wife, who I have loved from high school, but now realize that this life you want was never what I really wanted. I have found someone else who wants what I want, and I am going to try to get the kind of life I wanted. I'm sorry, but I have nothing to give you and the kid. I know you will take good care of her, because you are living the kind of life you always wanted. I know you will be fine. Again, I am sorry. Good-bye."

Unbelievable! She didn't just remember what it said, she'd memorized it.

"So!" I said, "he just wrote her a letter and took off."

"I don't know," Gloria said.

"Did you ask your mother about this?" I asked, feeling a little odd.

"Sure I did."

"And, what did she say?"

"What do you think she said?"

"I don't know. I'm waiting for you to tell me."

"She started crying, saying that she never wanted me to find out that he left her because of me. That he said he didn't want to have kids that early, and he was not ready for that kind of a life. Now, I ask you, what kind of man decides at the last minute that he doesn't want to have a kid when the baby is already here, huh?"

"I don't know, but he couldn't have been a good man to leave you and your mother like that. Look at you now, though. You're here in college and looking great. It's his loss, honey, not yours,"

I said, giving her shoulder a gentle squeeze. "I think your mom and you did okay."

Gloria looked at me and smiled, then laid her head on my chest.

I would hear many more stories like that throughout college. I discovered that many friends didn't have fathers at home growing up, yet they had made it to one of the best schools in the country and were doing very well in their studies.

I also ran into plenty of guys in college who spent a lot of their time bragging about how many girls they had gotten pregnant, bragging about how many kids they had running around somewhere. I instantly had a dislike for these guys.

I had no qualms about letting them know how I felt. I told them how stupid I thought they were for leaving some woman— or women, in some cases—to raise their kid, or kids, by herself, and how much I despised them for having the nerve to walk around crowing about it. I often wondered how these men would treat their children if they saw them. I suspected there would be a lot of shoving. I hoped not everybody's aunt would be able to intervene in time, like mine had.

Chapter 36

One of the most important things that growing up without a father had taught me was that it was extremely important to make sure you could take care of any child that you fathered. It had also taught me to think seriously about marriage, sex, and with whom I chose to have sex. Rhonda, however, had left her mark. I was determined that I'd never lose another girl because my no-good-father had turned me into some kind of prude.

I decided that I could dabble in sex, but that I would always be extremely careful. I did not want to impregnate any woman whom I did not intend to marry. Several of my high school class-mates couldn't wait, either, but they seemed to want to avoid being labeled sinners. They got married right out of school, but most were quickly divorced and remarried within three or four years. A few were even on their third marriage by that time. I learned that many of their divorces came as a result of arguments over finances.

I didn't want to get married without being in some kind of positive financial shape, and I definitely didn't want to marry someone I was not sure I really loved. I knew that, if and when I got married and had children, I just wanted to be the best husband and father I could be. I wanted to always be there for my children. I never wanted any of my children to ever believe that I didn't care. I also wanted to be able, as much as possible, to attend all the events in which they participated.

In college, I made my decisions about sex and dating based on my father leaving my mother, my sisters, and me. When I was in college I was kind of popular and had plenty of young women who were interested in me. I often found myself in some interesting situations with women and had to learn to have as much control as possible. I was always conscious of how I grew up. I didn't want to get some woman pregnant and have her decide to keep the baby when I didn't really want to be with her. I'm not saying that I was an angel; I was a long way from it. In fact, I slipped up just like other guys I knew.

I remember one night when I was dating Sabrina, she and I were going at it hot and heavy. Sabrina was a wonderful woman and had a beautiful body, I mean absolutely gorgeous, and I loved every inch of her. She and I had been good friends while we were in college and after college had kind of found our way back to each other. But this time we were more than just friends; we were actually seeing each other, exclusively, on a regular basis.

This particular night we were into each other and going at it real heavy, hugging and kissing and fondling each other. When we began to make love she whispered in my ear, "Carl, I want to have a baby."

This came out of nowhere, and I stopped, her legs still around my waist, and looked down at her. "What?"

She said it again: "I want to get pregnant—by you."

"Baby," I said, "we're not ready to have a baby. We're not married, and we have barely gotten into our careers." I stayed perfectly still. My mind started racing, and the words just flew out of my mouth. "You *are* still taking your birth control pills, aren't you?"

"Well," she said sheepishly, "I, kind of, well, missed a few days."

"What do you mean you kind of missed a couple of days?" I was struggling to get free of her legs. "What does that mean? How do you *kind of* miss a couple days of taking your pills?"

"Well, it wasn't intentional, really. I've just been busy at work, rushing out of the house in the morning, and I simply didn't think about it at night. Then I thought that since we were dating exclusively, perhaps it wouldn't matter if I got pregnant. And I would like to have your child."

My mind flashed to my mother trying to raise my sisters and me. I thought about the other women who were in my neighborhood with so many kids, mostly without fathers. Even the fathers who were around had difficulty making a decent living to support them.

Sabrina and I didn't finish our love making that night, but we did stay together for awhile. Eventually, she became busy with her job and I with mine, and we slowly drilled apart.

Chapter 37

I realized I knew many women who were trying to raise their children without a father in the home. Other people I knew, who had gotten married too soon and had started their marriage with kids, were having a rough time of it.

I sat there thinking, for what seemed like hours, about this situation. I had been in a similar situation many years ago and had promised myself not to ever slip up again. I was like most men, who often found themselves letting their little head, down below, get the best of their thinking. I was dating a fine little sister I had met one night while I was shopping at the local supermarket. I had not planned for things to get out of control.

Elizabeth lived not too far from the university and was working for a local accounting firm. She was quiet and had a great personality. I was still trying to finish up my engineering degree and really didn't need anything or anyone creating a distraction for me. We started talking, and I explained to her what my goals were. She said the exact same thing: that she had goals she wanted to complete. We agreed that we would keep things sort of casual and have fun. You know, go out to dinner and movies, and spend time talking. She would come over when I had to study and just be there. Sometimes she would be listening to music, or watching television or working on her plans for her own business.

We always used condoms—every time, no exceptions. Okay, once.

We were in bed, out of condoms. We both said I should get out of bed, go downstairs, and across the street to get some. There I was, sitting there with my girl, my love. I was naked, with my manhood sticking straight out, and my woman was telling me how much she loved me and wanted me. I couldn't bring myself to satisfy me or her right now. My thoughts were so clouded with my childhood and the struggles my mother had gone through to raise my sister and me. I was also thinking about the number of kids that I had too often seen in the neighborhood growing up like me, with no father around.

This, of course, was not particularly the case with Beth and me. I suppose that I loved her, but I simply wasn't ready to get her or anyone else pregnant, and I didn't want to mess up her career. I couldn't get beyond my situation and how things had happened with my mother and father. I was sure I would be the man that my father wasn't and do everything I could to make sure my child had the very best possible life, with me being a major part of it. But I wasn't sure I was prepared to do that right now.

Each time I tried to get up, she pulled me back. My mind kept telling me to get up. Beth finally said, "We can practice the pull-out method. If that doesn't work, I probably won't get pregnant this one time. But we may only be able to do it one time tonight."

I looked at her and said, "Nah, that's not going to work."

"Carlton, baby, it is cold outside, and I am burning up in here."

I have wished many a time that I had yielded to my own better judgment, and we had not made love that night. I attempted the pull-out, but Beth was holding on so tight …well, it happened, and it was too late. But, hey, it was only once, and we swore to keep a supply of condoms on hand forever after that. We convinced ourselves that she couldn't get pregnant that one time and remembered to keep the supply of condoms on hand.

Chapter 38

Beth had been given a new project at work. It was taking up a lot of time, and it was putting a lot of stress on her. She convinced herself—and me—that it was the stress that had interrupted her monthly cycle. Well, Occam's razor is painfully sharp. We found out soon enough that Beth's wayward period was caused by the most obvious of reasons.

The day she called me, I had just finished a major research project and was on top of the world. She said she needed to talk to me. It could wait, though, until after I'd celebrated a little with the fellows from the project team. She just didn't want to discuss it over the telephone. "Stop by after the party breaks up," she said.

I got to her apartment at about nine thirty and was feeling pretty good. When I walked in, she was sitting on the sofa, staring at nothing while Whitney Houston sang that she was saving all her love for me.

I kissed her on the lips. As I sat down beside her and put my arm around her shoulders, I realized she'd been crying. I thought maybe it was something that had happened at work, or bad news from home.

"I'm pregnant," she said, and the tears started again.

I didn't know what to do. I tried to recall all of the conversations that I'd had over the years with my mother, sisters, and women friends about what a man should and shouldn't do when a woman tells him he's gotten her pregnant.

I found that I couldn't move. I mean, I tried to get up because I wanted to walk back out the door; I wanted to hit myself and wake up in my apartment, in my own bed, as if this night wasn't here; but I was petrified. When I finally could speak, all I could muster was, "Are you sure? How could this have happened?"

"Remember the night it was so cold?" she said. "We were in bed, and you were out of condoms."

I really wanted to run and get out of there. There was no place for a child in my life right now. I also knew that Beth didn't have room in her life right now for a baby. We sat there for a minute, letting the music play and not saying anything, and then I asked, "Have you told your parents or your sister?"

"I haven't told my parents, but my sister and I talked today."

"How far along are you?"

"Five weeks."

"So, what are we going to do?" I asked.

"What do you mean?" she asked, a scared look on her face.

"Baby, you and I are not ready to bring a kid in to this world, are we?" I said, now feeling more than a bit uncomfortable. In the absence of grace and tact, I had nothing left but honesty. "Look," I said, "my friend Marcus got his girlfriend pregnant. They got married because of the baby. Neither of them had finished college, and now they are struggling, trying to finish school and take care of the baby."

I told her what Marcus had told me, that it just got bad with them, and they started arguing a lot. His wife had moved back home with her parents and was trying to finish at the university in her hometown. In the meantime, he was still in school and working a full-time job and a part-time job on the weekends to take care of the baby. His grades were suffering, and he feared there was a real chance he'd lose his scholarship.

"You want me to have an abortion?" Beth asked.

Oh, God. Was I actually asking her to end a life? Was I telling her that if she didn't, I wouldn't promise to stick by her?

I knew I wasn't ready for the responsibility of a kid. I cared about Beth, but I knew that she was not who I wanted to spend my life with. Yeah, that was about the size of it. I felt like a first-class heel. "Look Elizabeth," I whispered, "I don't want to hurt you, and I don't want something that has been beautiful to turn ugly. But I don't know how to stop it. I want you to be happy and comfortable, but I know, in this moment, you and I are not ready for this."

"Carlton, let's not beat around the bush. You don't want me to have this baby, and I am not ready to bring a child into the world where its father doesn't want it or me. I know, you care about me and enjoy making love to me, but the thought of marriage and kids—at least with me—is not on your agenda right now."

"I just don't think we are ready. We never talked about this."

"You're right, we never talked about this. We were too busy making love and never thought that this could happen. But it did, and I'm not sure if I want to let it go."

"Elizabeth, sweetheart," I said, "I know this is tough for you right now. You think that you want to have this baby, and you believe that all will be right with the world. But trust me, you will wake up and come to your senses and be mad at me for letting you go through with having this baby. You may hate me now for saying what I have been saying, but believe me I have seen this too many times before in my life, and it was never a happy ending. You and I need to put our feelings aside and think about this kid that is yet to be born, and what his or her life will be like with parents who brought him or her into the world too soon. Come on, we have to do what is right. I promise I will be with you every step of the way. I won't leave you to deal with this alone."

Chapter 39

It was a cold and rainy day in October. We had found a small clinic in her hometown. Her parents didn't know why we were there. Beth had given them some story about us coming down to see one of her friends who needed help with something. I can't remember the rest of the excuse.

There was the usual antiseptic smell of hospitals. In the waiting room were a lot of young women sitting along the walls. Some were reading magazines; others had their heads leaning on the shoulder of some guy. Still others sat alone and looked terribly sad. Beth signed in, and we took a seat in the waiting area.

They finally called her back, and she followed the nurse. She came out after about thirty or forty minutes.

"What happened?" I asked

"Nothing, I was talking with the nurse and the counselor. They wanted to make sure that I was sure this was what I wanted to do. They asked me if I wanted to have it and then give it up for adoption. Carlton, I thought about that for a few minutes while I was sitting there, but then I told them no. The nurse told me to come back out and sit down and think about this some more before they called me back."

I thought what we were doing was right, but I was having mixed thoughts and didn't know what to say. Some part of me wanted to grab her by the hand and walk out the door and never go back. Maybe, I thought, we *could* have a baby and do all that we needed to do, even though I was still in school and she had her career plans. We had not started out to be here, but maybe we could learn to love each other like husband and wife and make a good life for the child.

My mind was racing. Beth had her head on my shoulder, and I could hear her crying softly. We were here, and what happened in the next few hours would change her and change me. But I knew that it would be so much harder for her for a long while because I had heard women talk about how they felt after an abortion, and the many sleepless nights.

I sat, holding her. We didn't say much. Finally, the nurse came back for her, and she went in.

When Beth came out of the room, after what seemed like an eternity to me—God knows what it felt like to her—her face was blank. I rushed to her and asked if she was all right, but she didn't say a word; she just kept walking toward the door. We left the clinic.

I assumed she'd want to go home, to her parents' house, and headed in that direction.

"No, please take me home, back to my apartment."

The drive back to her apartment was almost three hours. She slept all the way. When we arrived, she seemed weak and I practically carried her inside and laid her on her bed.

"Would you please run me some water for a bath?" she asked weakly. "I need to take a bath."

I ran the tub almost completely full and helped her get undressed. I stayed in the room, just sitting and listening to some soft music. Through the door I could hear her crying and didn't know what to do. I did know she needed that time, and I decided not to disturb her. I must have dozed off for a minute and then I heard the bathroom door open. She walked out and got into her bed without saying a word.

I put the cover over her and lay down on top of the cover with my arm around her. I believed we had done the right thing, but I felt terrible and I knew she did, too. It was too late now; we could only look to the future.

Beth closed her eyes and went to sleep. I started praying and asked God to give her strength and to forgive us if we had erred in our decision. My heart was heavy because I knew that Beth would have to carry this burden much longer then I would, or, at least, she would think on this more often.

Afterward, we continued to see each other, but we were very careful and condoms were always on hand for lovemaking. After I finished school, I took a position out of town, and we both got busy with our careers and eventually went different ways. Whenever I was in town I would call, and we would meet and talk, but we didn't get back together.

One day, I got a call from Beth. She'd met someone, she said, and was getting married. All I could do was wish her well and say good-bye.

Chapter 40

Many years later, when I was grown and married and had a family of my own—the one that I had planned with the love of my life—I finally found out what had really happened between my mother and father.

Aunt Darlene told me one night when I was in Petersburg visiting her. I asked her why it had always seemed as if my grandmother, my father's mother, didn't like my mother and why she seemed so distant to my sisters and me.

She sat up in her chair. "Well, you were not the only ones she didn't like,"

"What do you mean?" I asked.

"Your grandmother didn't like Jennifer either, when she married Keith," she said.

Keith was my father's oldest brother. He had been married to my aunt Jennifer and had three children, just like my mother.

I was very interested in what my aunt had to say, so I said, "Don't stop now, please."

"Well, your grandmother never thought your mother was good enough for Leon. She never liked her and did everything she could to break them up."

"What do you mean? What could she do to break them up? And why would she?" I asked.

"Well, you could see it in her eyes at the wedding. She didn't say anything to your mother at the wedding, and when your sisters were born she never came to see them. She did come by once when your mother was pregnant with you. Your mother called me one night in tears and asked me to come over. When I got there her eyes were all swollen from crying. When I asked her what happened, she told that me your grandmother had stopped by, and they'd had an argument. According to your mother, your grandmother had accused her of trapping Leon by getting pregnant and having two babies, and now she was pregnant again.

"Your mother was so hurt that she wanted to leave right then. But I talked her into staying and trying to make it work, because she was pregnant with you and already had Louisa and Deidre."

"So, what happened?" I asked, starting to get angry all over again.

"Well, it was only six months after you were born. One day your mother came home, and all the furniture was gone and so was your father. She waited for him to come back to find out what had happened to the furniture, but he never returned that night. In fact, she didn't see him for about three days. She went to your grandmother's house to see if he was there, or if she had seen him, but his mother claimed that she didn't know where he was. None of his friends told her where your father was.

"Sometime early in the morning, we heard a knock at our door, and your mother was standing there with you in one arm and Deidre in another. Louisa was wrapped around her leg, and there was a bag on her back and a big suitcase sitting beside her.

"Your mother had gotten a cab and brought you and your sisters to our house with what little she could carry, or at least what was left."

I was sitting there in shock, with tears rolling down my face. I wiped the tears away and looked at my aunt.

"Several days later, Leon came to our apartment and asked for your mother," said Aunt Darlene. "When your mother came in the front room, your aunt Yvonne and I came with her. We were standing there, and your father started fussing at your mother. He started talking about how he felt like he was drowning; he said his mother had told him that if he was unhappy, he needed to get out and leave your mother; he said his mother had told him that he shouldn't have married her; he started blaming your mother for all his problems and cursing her.

"Well, your mother had a temper, and before we knew what was happening, she had grabbed your father and pushed him out the door. He fell back down the steps that led up to our apartment, and we thought that he must be seriously hurt.

"He struggled to get up, and, instead of leaving, he came back up the steps and rushed at your mother. He grabbed her by the arm with his fist balled up and was about to deliver a brutal blow.

But your Aunt Yvonne had gone and gotten your grandfather's shotgun. When we all turned, she had her finger on the trigger and was about to pull it. I grabbed it just as the gun went off. The buckshot hit the ceiling instead of your father. He fell to the floor and just sat there, looking kind of crazy and in shock. Your father got up, looking scared, and almost leaped down the steps to get out of there. Your mother and I got the gun from Yvonne and just sat there for a minute, looking at each other without saying a word."

I was riveted. "So what happened then?"

"Well, we all were scared to death, and we kind of continued to sit around for a while trying to figure out what had just happened. Your mother decided that night it was no use continuing a marriage that had no chance of surviving. She decided that she would take care of you guys by herself."

I sat there looking at my aunt and thinking about the story she had just told me, and I had to ask her, "How come my mother never told us about any of this?"

"It was something your mother wanted to forget, and your aunt Yvonne and I never wanted to remind her of such a bad time in her life."

Chapter 41

Sometimes we think that we have gotten rid of stuff that was painful, but it has simply lain dormant, waiting for the right time to resurface. My feelings about my father seemed to fall into this category.

It was around three o'clock, and it had been raining for about two hours when I realized that I had spent most of the day looking out the window and thinking. My thoughts had been mostly about my life and the many years I had struggled with issues surrounding my father. Here I was at forty-five, and the memories of his neglect, that I thought were long gone, were still in my head. His death had brought them back, or perhaps they had never really left.

I thought back to my high school graduation day. We were marching into the stadium; it was crowded with people, and I was excited, just like all my classmates. We had survived, what was for many of us, a rigorous academic curriculum that had prepared us well for college.

I had finished the very grueling curriculum in Scientific Collegiate, which required those who took this track to endure a lot of science and mathematics. When we finished, we were considered to be the best and the brightest of the high school. So I was confident on this day that I was ready for the world, especially for college.

As I sat with my classmates, I found myself turning my head from side to side, trying to get a good view of the people in the stands because I wanted to see if he was here. I spotted my mother, uncles, aunts, and my sisters, but I didn't see any of my relatives on my father's side. I didn't see any of them, and, most important to me, I didn't see my father. On this day I thought to myself, "He's not here; I don't see him. He could make up for all the misery that my mother, sisters and I endured over the years by being here tonight. He could make up in one evening for the eighteen years of watching my mother work her fingers to the bone to raise us, by just showing up for my graduation. Oh God, let him be here. If he's here, I can probably forgive him for missing my sisters' graduation. If he is here." I kept looking for him, but I didn't see him.

The speaker had finished his speech, the principal had called on the superintendent of schools to begin awarding the diplomas, and I was ready to graduate. As I walked across the stage, I saw my mother and sisters with their cameras ready to take my picture. At the very moment the principal put my diploma in my hands, their cameras went 'click' as they snapped my picture. Someone in the audience shouted, "Way to go Carl." Someone else said, "Hey, little Thomas. What's up?"

Walking back to my seat, I was as happy as I had ever been in my life. All my partners were there Edward, Ronald, and Tommy. Tommy hollered out, "Hey Carl, we made it man!" "Yeah, that's right, that's right, we're done," Ronald shouted. "We're on our way!" Edward was standing in one of the seats, waving his hat. He hollered, "Hey Carl, we're going to party tonight, man, for as long as we can."

I thought to myself, as I took my seat, even though he was nowhere to be found, at least not in the stadium, I was not going to let his absence mess up my special night. My mother and my family were happy for me. As for my boys, well, we were all floating on a cloud.

After the ceremony was over, I found my family and we headed home. My mother had planned a big party with all my relatives from her side of the family; however, I was not planning to stay around for the party, except maybe to collect a few gifts (money, I hoped) and to eat some of the wonderful food I saw all over the table.

My mother came up to me and hugged me so tenderly, then whispered in my ear, "I am so very proud of you, and know that, just as you have always done, you will continue to make me proud. I love you. I love you so very much. You have grown into a strong young man." My mother put a big stack of cards in my hands and said, "These are all for you."

I took a minute to open my cards, and most of them were filled with money. I mean fives, tens, and twenty-dollar bills. There were even two envelopes that had a couple of hundred-dollar bills in each. I stuffed them into my dresser drawer, grabbed a couple of pieces of chicken and started out the door when my sister Deidre grabbed my arm and pulled me into one corner of the living room. She looked at me and said, "You go get your friends and have yourself some fun. Louisa and I saw you looking around, but he didn't come. You let it go," she said, as her tears fell. "Let it go, you hear."

I almost started to cry, and she grabbed me gently and put her arms around me. "It's not worth it. Don't cry. This is your night, enjoy it."

I hugged my sister and went out the front door. Ronald and Edward were waiting for me, and we had a few stops to make before the night was over. This was my night and my mother's night because she had worked her tail off to get me here. My sisters had made it, and now I was finished with high school. It had been tougher for my mother, with me, probably because I was a boy. Being a woman, sometimes she didn't understand all that I was going through, but she was always willing to listen.

Sometimes I was even embarrassed to tell her certain things, so I would talk to my friends and occasionally my uncles, when I could find them. She told me what she could about sex, but most of the answers came from my friends and what I could get from my uncles. Some even came from books and the occasional girls that I dated. So, some of my early sexual knowledge was limited to that group of people.

As Ronald, Edward, and I were riding down the street, I thought about the wonderful job my mother had done; in fact, she had done an excellent job of raising me. I had never been in any trouble with the law and hadn't gotten into any academic or disciplinary trouble all through high school.

Of course, elementary school was a totally different story. I got into plenty of trouble there. In fact, I got more whippings because of the trouble I got into in the second, third, fourth, and fifth grades than I care to remember. As I got older, I realized that a lot of it was acting out and trying to get some attention. I missed my father and hated the fact that I didn't have one.

I know my mother knew our heartaches, but she did not pamper us—and she took no mercy on bad behavior, whatever the reason. She had no problem at all whipping my behind, or my sisters. Even though neither one of them got into trouble at school, they got into their share of trouble at home.

In fact, I used to hate it when the teachers found out who I was because they knew both of my sisters and would waste no time telling me, "Your sisters were both model students and very smart. What is your problem?" I, of course, would always have something prepared for them. I would say, "Well, since I am not my sisters, and I am a man, maybe you should go and get them." This, of course, would earn me a trip to the principal's office and, later, a whipping when I got home. But all and all, it was okay growing up. At least now I was finished with high school, and I was on my way to college.

Chapter 42

Sitting at my father's funeral, listening to the soloist as she was singing, I thought so much about what and where my father would spend eternity. I never heard anybody say that my father was a Christian. I never knew if he was actually a member of any church, or even went to church, except for various funerals that I knew he had attended. So I had no clue. Regardless of what he had lacked in being a father to my sisters and me, my Biblical teaching and church upbringing would not let me wish him any ill will. I really didn't want him to spend eternity in Hell. He was still a child of God, and I had been taught to want all God's children to be with Him for eternity. Whether he would make it or not was not my call.

As the soloist finished, I noticed on the program that there was a section for comments from family and friends. I thought to myself, "I certainly hope no one is expecting me to say anything. If they need one of his children, then Louisa is going to have to do it. I am not saying a thing."

Immediately after that thought, my sister leaned over to me and said, "If one of his children has to say something, you are the chosen one." She sat back and looked straight ahead without blinking or saying anything else.

"No way," I said. "It should be you. You spent the most time with him. I am the last person to say something about him."

Louisa didn't respond but tilted her head toward me this time with a slight smile on her face. I reached over and grabbed her arm and said, "Don't do this to me."

"Do what to you?" she said, still grinning. "You're a big boy now."

"Right. Oh, now I'm a big boy."

She smiled.

I watched very carefully because I wanted to see who was going to get up and speak about my father and exactly what would they say. As I sat there beside my sister, waiting to see who would get up, a man finally stood up and headed toward the podium. I had no idea who he was, but from my sister's facial expression, I got the feeling she recognized him.

What he said was interesting, and I listened very closely to his remarks.

"My name is Levi Johnson," he said with a slightly husky voice. It almost seemed as if he had been drinking alcohol by the slurring of his words. "I have lived on the Height for the past sixty years. I have known Leon for almost all of those years. Leon never bothered anybody. He always stayed pretty much to himself, but he played cards around Elsie's house and drank a little bit. For the most part, he was a pretty good guy. I'm real sorry that he is gone, but I know he will be okay. I wish his family the very best. Thank you." And he walked slowly back to his seat.

What a profound statement. He was a good man and never bothered anybody.

"Well, buddy," I thought to myself, "you forgot to talk about his children that he totally neglected, and his wife, so what in the hell were you talking about? He was a good man! I guess neglecting your children and abandoning your wife does not count. I guess this is what was to be expected?"

My aunt Lilly was next. She got up to speak on behalf of the family. "Leon was my middle brother, who my mother loved. Sometimes we even thought that she loved him more than the rest of us. He was what we called the one who kept the rest of us awake. He didn't like being like the rest of us he liked spending his time on whatever interested him, and most of the time that was just plain old relaxation."

Yeah, a fellow really needs a break after long hours on the dole and hitting the bottle.

"Leon never really liked working. He preferred to spend his time sitting in the sun during the summer and by the fire during the winter, talking with his friends," she continued. "He never bothered anyone and was always pleasant to everyone he met. So, what do you say about a brother when he has gone on home? We thank God for the short time he gave you to us. We wish you peace in your rest. May God keep you in His care."

After she finished, I leaned over to my sister and said, "You'd think the guy was a gentle saint. Obviously, I've misjudged him all these years, poor soul."

Louisa nearly snorted aloud. "I was trying to figure out where she got that crap from," she hissed. "I guess she didn't say anything about his family because they didn't think he had one, or at least one that he cared enough about to acknowledge. Well, who cares now, anyway?" We both kind of laughed a little, and then we saw the minister get up again. The moment that I had dreaded came. The minister said, "Now we will hear from Mr. Thomas's children."

I was in shock and could not move. Louisa was practically pushing me out of the pew. Apparently, though, it wasn't my cue after all.

Curtis was heading for the pulpit. I was so relieved. He got up and said, "My father was a good man, and I, for one, am going to miss him. He tried to get me to do the right thing, but for some reason as I was growing up, I didn't listen and got myself into a lot of trouble. He and I spent time together just talking about life and what was going on in the world. I will miss him and realize that he has gone home too soon. I thank all of you for coming. To my brother and sister, I am glad you guys are here."

Curtis took his seat, and the minister came back and said, "Now we will hear from his other children."

Chapter 43

I couldn't move, and my sister did nothing. True to her word, she did absolutely nothing and waited for me to get up and say something. I, with all my public speaking experience, could not move. I was waiting to see if someone else was going to get up. I guess I expected that there were some other kids that my father had fathered who might all of a sudden show up and claim him.

The minister made his call again. I forced myself up and headed toward the pulpit. Just as I was about to step up, I slipped, but I regained my balance and grabbed onto the lectern. I turned and looked out into the audience and stood there for a minute. I thought about what my mother had always said, "If you can't say something good about somebody, don't say anything." At that moment, I wanted to abandon her teaching on this matter. I wanted to tell these people exactly how I felt, tell them how we had been treated by this man lying here. They all called him my sisters' and my father. I wanted them to know about all the years I had suffered from his neglect, and the fact that my sister Deidre was so bothered that she didn't even want to come home for his funeral. Yes, I needed to abandon my mother's teaching because they needed to know that you don't treat your kids like crap all their lives, then expect that they will be there for you at the end of your life.

These people seated here needed to hear that no man should abandon his family and not ever check on them to see how they really are doing, or whether they are living okay. Standing there thinking about this, I was getting angry about some of the stuff that I thought was gone. They needed to know, and I wanted to tell them, that no man can have a son, or sons, and never once spend any time with them. Or just because the mother and he are unable to work things out, he decides that the woman he has fathered the child with is not who he wants. Or that his wife is no longer who he wants, so he leaves her and abandons their child or children in the process, not caring how he, or she, or they, will grow up. I needed to calm myself down, because I was getting so emotional standing there. I knew that I had to say something, but what should I say?"

I kept looking out in the audience. I'm not sure how long I had been standing there. I looked over at Louisa and she smiled kindly to me and mouthed something that I took to mean, "What are you waiting for? You can do this."

I did everything that I had been taught in law school and in public speaking class to do. I put my hands on each side of the lectern to make sure I would not be using my hands to talk. I stood up straight and tried to compose myself. I opened my mouth and nothing came out. I took another stab at it and, before I knew it, said, "You know, I have been taught all my life by my mother, God rest her soul, that I should only say something good about a person, and if I couldn't, I shouldn't say anything. What I'm about to say may not particularly please my mother, but she's not here. I know that only God calls his children home, and what my father did, or didn't do, had nothing to do with her going home early. But my mother worked herself to death to take care of her three children after my father decided that he no longer wanted that responsibility. I watched her work day and night to provide for her children. My father never came around to see how we were doing, and he lived not more than one or two miles away most of the time. He never gave us anything. I am not sure if any of you know how hard it is for a little boy never to see his father, or when he does, he receives nothing from him no sense of love or caring, no money to put into his pocket, no teaching or training to be a man, no words of encouragement. Then he doesn't even bother to show up to your high school graduation.

"All the memories I have of my father, who is lying here, are bad, nothing good. I know there must have been some good in him, because some of you have spoken well about him. My sister and I were sitting there, trying to figure out who you all were talking about because we didn't know that man. My mother never prevented my father from seeing us. I even remember that she always encouraged us to go and see our grandparents, then asked us if we had seen our father. I guess what my father forgot is that you can leave your wife, or even your girlfriend, but if you have kids, you can't leave them. Or, at least, you shouldn't. They are still your responsibility.

"No, I can't say that I will miss my father because, in truth, I never had a father. He was someone my mother told us was our father, and people in the neighborhood referred to him as such. He never acted in any way as I believe a father should have, so what is it that I, as a son, should say about this man lying here on this day?

"Perhaps, as I look back, there is one thing that my father did for me besides assisting my mother into bringing me into the world. He got out of the way and let my mother raise us. I've never been happy about not having a father, like a lot of my friends, or like we always saw on television. I guess my father realized, that perhaps, he had nothing to offer my sisters and me, so he left and let my mother have that responsibility.

"But as I look at my stepbrother sitting there, who was with my father and was influenced by him, I realize that he has been in and out of jail more times than I can count. I am not saying that it was my father's fault or influence, but it is rather strange that he looks much older than his years on earth, although he is much younger than I. He has several kids that he can't, or doesn't, support. With all this being said, I thank God that He gave my mother the strength to raise my sisters and me. She kept us in church, away from the bad stuff and away from my father's influence.

"Neither my sisters nor I have ever been in trouble, nor have we been hooked on drugs or alcohol. We've tried to be good

Christians. I guess my father did one thing for his children that he never really knew he was doing and that was leaving us with my mother. So, today, I guess it is fitting that I thank him for his ability to leave, even though most of my life I hated him for leaving us. I was a son, and I needed my father.

"I have my own family now, with a wife and two wonderful children. I got married late because I wanted to be ready to love my wife and children when I had them. I wanted to be sure I was ready to make the commitment that a father has to make to his wife, and especially to his children. I believe this commitment involves being there for them, caring for them, providing financially for them, and supporting them mentally. I believe it involves demonstrating that you love them by hugging them periodically and attending their school and sports events. It means being there for them, even if the love relationship between the man and woman, or husband and wife, has failed. The love relationship with the children must remain. Yes, I am a better man, able to love my children unconditionally because of my mother and father's situation, especially his neglect. My commitment has always been to do the very best for my family, regardless of the situation."

When I finished, I looked over at my sister, who looked as if she had been crying. I said, "I am very sorry if this is not what you all expected. But what did you expect a son or daughter to say about a father who was never a father? I thank you all for coming and for listening. I sincerely hope that if any of you have children, and you are not doing the very best for them, that you will take my words seriously and make the change today.

"If any of you men have children that you have not seen, go find them. Hug them and tell them that you love them. Promise that you will do better. Find the mother of your children and try to make amends. Apologize if necessary, but ask if you can start seeing your children again. If you owe back child support, work out a plan of action to take care of it. You fathered the child, or the children, so you must do what is right for them. The two of you may not be able to work out your differences, but please don't make your problems the children's problems. All children need their fathers, and boys especially need their fathers. I thank you all for coming to say good-bye to my father, and I wish you all the very best."

As I stepped down from the pulpit, I looked at Louisa, feeling rather bad that I had said all that. In my distraction, I slipped. I tried to catch myself, but I hit my head on the front pew.

Chapter 44

When I could clear my head, I looked up and, for some reason, things were kind of cloudy. I saw someone standing there and I asked, "What happened?"

"Sir, are you all right?" a woman asked.

"Yeah, I'm fine," I said. "Where am I?" I quickly noticed that I was sitting on an airport bench, and there were several people standing around. I looked at them more closely. They were airline personnel. The woman who was there said to me, "Sir, are you sure? Do we need to get you some help?"

"What?" I asked.

"Are you okay? Do you still need the ticket?"

"Where am I? What are you talking about?" I asked, still confused by their presence and still trying to clear my head and get my bearings straight.

"Sir, you are at JFK Airport in New York," said a man standing beside her. "Do you need some help?"

"Wait," I said. "Wait just a minute."

I looked at them and thought to myself, "What happened? What did I say? Why can't I remember?" Just then the airline attendant said, "Sir, do you want the ticket?"

"What ticket?" I asked. "What are you talking about?" I looked at the woman's name tag and noticed that her name was Linda Anderson.

"The ticket you asked me for, to Memphis," she said.

"No, I need a ticket to Richmond, Virginia. I've got to get to my father's funeral in Petersburg, Virginia. Do you have a bereavement fare?"

"Yes, we do. If you are all right, let's move back over to the counter so I can help you. I need to get to the computer, okay?"

"Okay, but what's the cost for the bereavement fare? My father died, and I need to get to his funeral. I have to get there early to meet my sister. She's flying in from Texas at ten o'clock this morning."

"Sir, we have a couple of flights going out today," she said.

"Okay, that's perfect because I promised my sister that I would meet her. The funeral is at 1:00 PM."

"Okay, Mr. Thomas, that will be $625."

"Is that the bereavement fare?" I asked. "What is the normal rate?"

"Well, Mr. Thomas, since it is a one-day purchase, it costs about $1,060."

"Wait a minute," I said. "What do you mean, a one-day rate?" I asked.

"Your flight leaves this afternoon at 4:30 and will arrive at about 6:45 PM. You will be there in time to meet your sister in the morning; however, if you would like a later flight, I have something leaving later tonight at 8:00 PM and it will get you there at around 9:30 PM."

"Wait, wait, wait," I said. "What are you talking about? What do you mean, I'm not flying to Richmond this afternoon or tonight? I have to meet my sister in Petersburg, Virginia at ten o'clock this morning, and Petersburg is about thirty minutes from Richmond."

"Mr. Thomas, are you okay?"

"Yes, I'm okay, I just need you to put me on the next flight to Richmond, so I can meet my sister and get to my father's funeral."

"Mr. Thomas, I'm sorry, but exactly when is your father's funeral?"

"What in the world are you talking about? I have been standing here, talking to you for the past thirty minutes, and you were supposed to be booking me a flight to get to Richmond this morning."

"Mr. Thomas, would you excuse me for a minute."

Chapter 45

The airline attendant disappeared into the back and returned with another person, dressed in the same kind of blue and red attire, only his was a blue suit and red tie. "Hello, Mr. Thomas, I'm Irvin Mitchell, the desk supervisor. Are you okay, and is there someone we can call?"

"Excuse me. Why do I need you? All I need is a ticket to Richmond, Virginia, so I can get there before 10:00 AM or at least by 12:00 noon because I have to meet my sister at the funeral home so we can bury my father today. The funeral is at 1:00 PM. today, and all I need is a ticket. She has already told me the price. May I have my ticket so I can catch the flight?"

"Well, Mr. Thomas, we are here to assist you in getting your flight, but according to Ms. Anderson, just a few minutes ago you slipped and fell and hit your head. She said that you were having some problems focusing and seemed to be a little confused about some things. Are you sure you are okay?"

"Why does everyone keep asking me that? No, I am not confused. I just need the ticket I asked for."

"Well, Mr. Thomas, you see, that's the problem."

"Why is that a problem? You don't have a flight?"

"No sir, that's not the problem."

"Excuse me. What is your name?"

"Oh, I'm sorry; I thought I told you my name when I came up. I'm Irvin Mitchell, the desk supervisor."

"No, I don't recall. But can I get my ticket?"

"Well, sir, as I told you, that is the problem."

"Okay. What's the problem, sir? Or is it Mr. Mitchell? Why can't I have my ticket?"

While I was talking with Mr. Mitchell, two other people appeared at the desk. One was an airport security officer. I'm starting to get bothered so I say, "Look, what's going on? I just need a ticket to get to the funeral, okay?"

The officer stepped up and said, "Mr. Thomas, would you come with me?"

"Officer, have I done something?" I asked.

"Sir, I just need you to come with me for a minute," he replied.

"Is there a problem?" I asked again.

"We're not sure, Mr. Thomas," he said.

"What do you mean?" I asked, getting a little more concerned.

"Mr. Thomas, would you please just step over here for a minute? I need to ask you some questions."

I followed the officer and the supervisor, Mr. Mitchell, over near the security area, away from the counter.

"Mr. Thomas, do you know what day it is?" the officer asked.

"Yes, of course, I know what day it is. Today my sister and I are going to bury my father. Today is November 8, 2005, and we are burying my father at one o'clock this afternoon."

"Mr. Thomas, you are right; today is November 8, 2005, but you can't get a flight to Richmond at 8:00 AM or 9:00 AM or anything like that today. Because, Mr. Thomas, it is 3:47 PM."

I was standing there listening to this officer; Ms. Anderson, the airline attendant; the supervisor; a new officer, and another person who had just joined the group standing there looking at the officer like he had totally lost his mind. I said, "What are you talking about? It is only 7:30 in the morning."

"Mr. Thomas, are you sure you are all right?" Mr. Mitchell asked.

"Mr. Thomas, I think we need to call someone," the officer said again.

"No. I mean, you don't need to call anyone," I said, looking around and trying to think clearly. "I'm really okay."

"No, Mr. Thomas, we are not sure you are okay because it is 3:55 in the afternoon, and, apparently, you were supposed to be somewhere at 12:00 noon today. It appears that you can't remember what happened to the rest of your day. Sir, it is late afternoon now."

My legs almost gave out so I used the counter to hold myself up. I looked up at the clock and, sure enough, it was actually 4:00 PM. Suddenly, I am not sure where I have been for the last seven or more hours. I thought to myself, "I need to get out of here because these people think I'm crazy, and with the current situation in the country, being in an airport where the airline staff, not to mention the police, thinks you are crazy is surely not a good sign."

I straightened myself up and tried to get myself together. I decided I needed to come up with some kind of explanation that would convince these people that I was okay, so I could get out of there.

After some fast talking, I seemed to convince them I was okay and had a friend in the city I could visit, so they let me walk out. I grabbed a taxi and headed downtown to the Sheraton Hotel. Luckily for me, the hotel still had my room, and I checked back in. Before heading up to the room, I bought a glass of white wine. As soon as I walked in my room, I called home. The telephone rang, and my wife answered. "Hello."

"Hi baby, how are you doing?"

"Hi, darling," she said. "I'm glad you called. I was thinking about you. I'm okay, it has just been a busy day, but I'm fine. I was worried about you and wanted to know whether you had made it back home, or if you had decided to stop by and see me and the kids."

"Well, baby, I wanted to, but I'm not sure what's going on with me right now."

"What do you mean?"

"Well, some strange things have been happening, and I'm not sure how to deal with them right now; I need to talk with my sister. Once I have done that, I will know more. So wait until I talk to her, and I will get back with you."

"Okay, I'll wait. Are you okay about your father?"

"I'm not sure right now. Everything is still kind of cloudy, you know. But that's enough about me. How're the kids doing? Are they okay?"

"I think so, but they are worried about you. I told them that your father died, and they wanted to know how, and whether you were okay and if we were going to the funeral."

"What did you tell them?

"I told them that you and your sisters were working with your aunt to figure out how you were going to handle things, and how it was difficult to work it out because it was so far away, and you were in Memphis."

"How did they take it?"

"Devon was okay, but a little quiet. Patria was more bothered and stayed in her room most of the evening."

"I'll talk to both of them later and explain things. I love you, and I will call you tomorrow, when I get back. I'm very tired, and I am going to take a shower and go to bed. Kiss the kids for me. I love you."

After I hung up, I immediately called my sister. I didn't tell my wife what happened at the airport, because I was still confused by it myself. But I knew I needed to talk with my sister to get some answers, and fast. I dialed her number and the voicemail came on. "Hey Lou, this is your brother, call me back as soon as you get this message. I need to talk with you now. It is extremely important. Bye."

I sat down in the chair near the window and looked out at the lights of New York City. I had always loved looking at the lights in downtown New York, especially on Broadway. I sat there trying to figure out what had happened and where my day had gone.

At least an hour passed before I heard my cell phone ringing. I picked it up, and it was my sister. I was glad to hear her voice. I was not sure what had happened today and what had happened with my father's funeral. I didn't tell my wife the total truth about my day, because the last thing I wanted to do was worry her about what I was going through because I was not sure. Besides, she had the kids, and right now that was enough for her to deal with.

"Hey Lou," I said. "Where are you?"

"What do you mean, where am I? I'm still in Texas."

"What are you doing there?" I asked in disbelief. She should have been in Richmond by now.

"What do you mean?"

"I thought we were going to meet in Petersburg at Leon's funeral."

"Carlton, what in the world are you talking about?"

"Well, I thought we were going to meet in Petersburg at the funeral home."

"Carlton, please get a grip on yourself."

"Lou, I'm trying, but something is not right."

"What are you talking about?" she asked. "What's not right?"

Chapter 46

When I woke up, I was lying across my bed. Apparently, I had fallen asleep in my clothes. It was about six o'clock in the evening, and it was raining outside. I was not sure how long I had been asleep. All I could remember was that I was sitting, waiting for time to pass, hoping that the funeral was over, and he was finally in the ground. "What day was it?" I thought to myself. "Did I ever make it to New York to the Thurgood meeting?" I wasn't sure. I was supposed to be there the day before father's funeral, but, well, I really couldn't remember. At this point, there were more important things to think about.

They buried my father today and I was not there to say goodbye, but I wanted him in the ground. I'm not sure why this was so important to me. My sister had called yesterday while I was in New York and told me that she had decided not to attend the funeral because she hadn't ever really wanted to go, but felt that she should have gone out of respect.

Diedre had made it clear to us that she was not even considering coming from Germany for a funeral, since she couldn't have cared less if Leon lived or died. To her, Leon was a memory that she wanted to forget.

I remembered having an earlier conversation with Louisa. She'd said, "Carlton, all the years I have been talking with the doctors about Leon's medical problems, I have been miserable. But because we were his children and I knew that you and

Deidre, especially Deidre, wanted nothing to do with him really, since I was the oldest I felt that it was my responsibility. "But Carlton," Louisa said, "being responsible for him was a major burden for me, knowing that he had never been a real father or cared about us at all. I always thought about mother and felt bad because here I was taking care of him, and he had never done anything for us.

"I couldn't go to the funeral because I didn't want to see a bunch of folks who never cared whether we lived or died—the folks who never once came to see how we were living. I just can't go. So if you want to go, it's okay, but I can't be there with you, and you know that Deidre is not coming."

"Louisa, I always thought that you needed our father more than I, or even Deidre, did."

"I did once, you know. I even used to cry for him, hoping that he would show up or just be there. I wanted so much for him to just say that we were important to him. But when that never happened, I told myself that I had to get over it and move on. So, my dear brother, I moved on many years ago. Everything I did, from that point, was simply out of obligation, or trying to live by the teachings of our mother when she taught us to always treat people with respect, and that he was our father, although not a very good one or one that cared, we still had to treat him with respect."

"Hey girl, I never thought you felt that way about him. I always thought just the opposite. Are you okay?"

"Yeah, Carlton, I'm okay and I'll be fine. But how about you?"

"I'm not sure about me, but I'll get over this because I still have you, Deidre, Mildred, and my two beautiful children. You know, Lou, I thought that I had put all this behind me, and as long as you didn't mention his name or what was happening with him, I was fine," I said. "But for me, you know, a father is always someone that most men or guys want to, at least, know about. Even if they don't see him, men still think about their fathers."

"I think you're right, Carl. With Eric, even when he was a little boy, he wanted to know his father. His face would just light up when his father came around. So I do understand."

I was relieved to hear that from Louisa. "I guess for me, you know, growing up knowing that he was somewhere in the city, but that he never showed any interest in seeing us, was really hard for me. And even though you, and especially Deidre, didn't talk about it much, I know it hurt you two, also."

"Yeah, it did, but we had to learn to let it go."

Chapter 47

I sat in my favorite chair in the living room of my apartment and thought, "My father is dead and buried, and I missed it." My wife, Mildred, and my two children were back in Northern Virginia, and I was here alone. I had come down to work on this assignment that was supposed to last only six months, but it had already been eight, and I was ready to go home. I needed my wife and children, especially now.

I hoped that there was someone at my father's funeral who would say something good about him and his children, or at least remember that he had children. I can only hope that his other son, Curtis, showed up. I wonder what kind of service it was. What did his friends say about him? Did they mention his kids, or did anyone really even think of us?

Then again, what does it matter now? None of my aunts or uncles on my father's side had ever really thought of us seriously enough to care how we were living. No, not even our grandmother had thought enough of us to see how we were doing when we were growing up. One would think that a mother or father would make their son go and see about his kids, or at least check to see how their grandchildren were doing. It's disheartening to realize that there are grandmothers out there who do not care about their grandchildren because they dislike the children's mother. But it does happen. I know because it happened to my sisters and me. I had not one memory of my father's mother ever coming to our house or even telling us that she loved us. We never got any hugs or kisses from her, or from any of my aunts on my father's side of the family. This had always bothered my sisters and me, and we used to talk about it among ourselves. Eventually, we just stopped worrying about it.

Chapter 48

What do I say to people when they ask me about my father's funeral? Most folks expect that you will attend your father's funeral and be emotionally upset by his death. So what do I say?

I reached over to the coffee table where all the cards I had received were stacked, picked them up, and began reading some of them. One of the first cards I picked up read, "With Heartfelt Sympathy for Your Family's Loss," and it continued with, "Where there is love, there is hope, and where there is hope, there is strength." Inside, the card read, "May the love you feel for each other surround you now and ease your sorrow."

Beautiful! Another read on its front, "The Lord Is with You." Inside, it read, "In God's Word and in His Love we can find the comfort and strength we need to see us through our sorrow."

And yet another read, "May God Comfort You," and the inside read, "Blessed are those who mourn, for they will be comforted. May it be a source of inner strength to know that there's a loving God watching over you, and that throughout this time of need, He'll stay close by your side."

I'm a guy who had a father but never had a dad. He was there, up the street and around the corner, but when we didn't have food, he didn't come; when we didn't have water, he didn't come; when I fell down, he didn't come; when I almost died, he didn't come; when my sisters and I graduated from high school, he didn't come; when I graduated from college, he didn't come;

when Deidre graduated from the basic training and AIT school, he didn't come; when we got married, he didn't come. No matter what, my father never came.

All the cards were beautiful, and I really appreciated my co-workers, church members, and friends for thinking of me and my family during this time.

But they don't know the real story. They know nothing of my struggle to become a decent man, to be a good husband and father, without ever having seen a good husband and father up close.

I pray God will forgive me if I have erred in my feelings toward one of his children.

My father, Leon Thomas, died this morning. So what?